Slowly Heather began to remove Deila's gown. "I want to see your beautiful body." Next, Heather took off her own garment. "Now! I can feel you better against me." Naked they embraced, body to body, warm flesh blending as one.

Lightly Heather caressed Delia's breasts and round stomach. "You're so fragile, like a jewel. My precious jewel." She kissed her forehead, tasting the saltiness of her skin with the tip of her tongue. The trembling of the girl's body imparted the message she wanted to know. Fired with passion, Heather stroked the tapering tights inside and out . . .

The Black and White of It

Ann Allen Shockley

The Black and White of It

Ann Allen Shockley

The Naiad Press Inc.
1987

Printed in the United States of America

THE BLACK AND WHITE OF IT was issued first by Naiad Press in 1980 with two fewer stories included. "The Mistress and the Slave Girl" and "Women in a Southern Time" are the new stories in this edition. The former has also appeared in THE LEADING EDGE (1987) and the latter appeared in the magazine, FEMINARY, V. IX #1&2. "A Special Evening" first appeared in SISTERS, August, 1973 and "A Meeting of the Sapphic Daughters" first appeared in SINISTER WISDOM 9, Spring, 1979.

Cover design by Women's Graphic Center
Typesetting by Sandi Stancil

ISBN 0-930044-96-7

BOOKS BY ANN ALLEN SHOCKLEY

LOVING HER (Naiad)
SAY JESUS AND COME TO ME (Naiad)
THE BLACK AND WHITE OF IT (Naiad)
LIVING BLACK AMERICAN AUTHORS: A BIOGRAPHICAL
 DIRECTORY (with Sue P. Chandler) (Bowker)
A HANDBOOK OF BLACK LIBRARIANSHIP (with E. J. Josey) (Libraries
 Unlimited)
AFRO-AMERICAN LITERARY FOREMOTHERS: A DOCUMENTATION,
 1746-1933 (G. K. Hall) (forthcoming)

ABOUT
ANN ALLEN SHOCKLEY: AN ANNOTATED PRIMARY AND
 SECONDARY BIBLIOGRAPHY by Rita B. Dandridge. (Greenwood)

CONTENTS

The Black and White of It

Ann Allen Shockley

SPRING INTO AUTUMN

Seated half turned at her desk, Penelope Bullock stared absently out the window, watching the students hunched against the cold, hurrying across campus. The day was bleak and thick with a dreary hovering grayness that did not help her mood. January was a particularly depressing month to her. An anniversary commemorating a year ago when Claire walked away after the eight years of all they had shared together. Without any visible signs of regret, Claire moved out of the apartment, leaving the furniture and Frizzle, a black and white curly haired three-year-old mutt.

Penelope was glad that Claire had left Frizzle, for he made being alone not exactly alone. The dog loved her and offered the nearest thing to human companionship. At least he was waiting when she returned home from work in the evenings. Aside from Frizzle to help combat the chilling silence of the apartment, she brought home papers to grade and plunged into completing her book on John Milton.

At the age of forty-two, Penelope had decided that there was nothing else for her to do but concentrate on her work. She had no intimate friends and was too shy to go where she might meet others like herself. This would entail making approaches, reversing the role she had assumed throughout the years with Claire. At this point in time, she had to be the hunter instead of the prey. Who wanted a woman her age, especially like herself? She was much too thin, the brown hair turning so mousy that she had to have it tinted a richer color every month. Only recently, she had to have a partial plate put in to replace the teeth her dentist told her had to be extracted. Gazing now at the fresh faces of youth passing outside, the thought numbed her that the prime of her life had been occupied by Claire, only to come to this. She sighed. Why lament? Husbands left wives didn't they after an accumulation of years. Wasn't life just a gamble?

A knock sounded, trespassing upon her reflections. She frowned, turning around in the swivel chair to confront the closed door. "Come in."

The girl came in smiling, transmitting an aura of brightness into the cluttered cubicle of the room. Her office was similar to all the others in the Humanities Building except for the department chairpersons. It was small, furnished with two hard chairs, a metal file cabinet and a worktable with an ancient typewriter. Once a year during the fall, just before the Board of Trustees met, the high bare walls were freshened with the same slimy green paint.

"Dr. Bullock?"

Her visitor had a strong pungent odor of a winter's day. Cold was embedded in the ruddiness of her wind-pressed cheeks. She wore the typical student attire of faded bell-bottom jeans and a short red and black checkered wool pantcoat with the collar turned up to protect the part of her neck where a black knit cap didn't cover.

"Yes?" Penelope's frown deepened. She had no student conferences scheduled for today. The girl was an intrusion upon her afternoon, and worst of all, her thoughts.

"I'm Jenifer Downs. Everybody calls me J. D.," she added, coming closer. "I've been assigned as a student assistant to you."

"Oh?" Another bureaucratic mix up. "It was my understanding that Sally Lake would be assigned to me again. She's worked with me for the last two semesters." Besides, she had become accustomed to Sally. The girl was a good worker who came and went quietly about her business. It was the caliber of work that mattered to Penelope. She did not feed relationships.

"I know, Dr. Bullock, but Sally didn't come back this semester. Her mother's sick," J. D. explained softly, showing she had sensed the woman's disappointment.

"I see—" Penelope was dismayed. Once more the stableness of her existence was being challenged. She would have to train someone else all over again. Nothing stayed constant with her; no one ever seemed to remain.

"Here are the times when I can be available," J. D. said, handing her a piece of paper with the hours on it.

"I'll go over this and let you know tomorrow when is best for me," Penelope said, placing the schedule on top of a small hill of papers. "Of course, you're an English major." She always requested majors in her field. Somehow, she couldn't recall the girl's being in any of her classes.

"No—math."

Again disruption! Her mouth betrayed her by emitting a gasp. "But I always request *English* majors. I thought it was *understood.*"

J. D.'s blue eyes noted her distress and clouded with sympathy. "I'm sorry, Dr. Bullock, but I'm the only student left to be assigned. *I'd* rather work in the math department too. Only I wasn't here last semester and this is all they could offer me." Her voice softened: "I can type, spell and what I can't spell, I know how to look up in the dictionary. I worked as a typist off and on for two years before I came here."

Penelope leaned forward to examine her more closely. Her round spirited face seemed more mature than most of the students. She appeared to be about twenty-three or four. She was short and chunky with stubby fingers tipped by closely clipped nails. Her mouth was a thread-like incision above almost a double chin. J. D. met her inspection squarely, standing back on her heels, taking her in too. Feeling subjugated by the locked stare, Penelope quickly shifted her eyes to a distant point beyond. "I believe you are a good typist, Miss Downs—" she said stiffly, hoping the girl would get the implication of formality in her office. She did not call students by their first names. "How are you classified?"

"I'm a senior—at last!" she grinned. "It's taken me five years off and on to get there. I'm putting myself through school, so I have to work and go part-time. Only now, with this job, I have enough saved to make it through this semester full-time."

"How nice." The girl had perseverance and determination. Those traits should show up in her work. "Can you come in tomorrow at two?"

"Sure can—" J. D. smiled.

Penelope noticed the straight even white teeth and envy shuddered her. Unconsciously her tongue slipped over the partial.

"What will I be doing, Dr. Bullock?"

"Typing, filing, some research. Odds and ends."

"Whatever *you* say. See you tomorrow."

"Goodday—" Penelope said crisply, resenting what she considered familiarity creeping into J. D.'s tone.

When the door closed, Penelope reached for a cigarette in her drawer. She kept the pack there to prevent students in conference with her from asking for one. The casualness of a cigarette could produce an air of sociableness. She believed in holding herself aloof. Lighting the cigarette, she inhaled deeply, drawing in a suction of relief. She brought the square glass ashtray with the name Oglethorpe College—1898 closer to her. All faculty members were given Oglethorpe ashtrays. This was to help promote the name of the small private college located on the outskirts of the city. It was a perfect working set up for her, for she could get home in thirty minutes. Back to the anonymity of the city where she could live as she had with Claire, hidden away in the cavernous mouth of another existence.

Claire operated a boutique, an expensive little shop near the downtown section. Their relationship had been ideal, at least to her, until the gradual crumbling, and finally Claire's announcement: "I'm leaving—there's someone else."

The confession had not startled her. Why should it? She had been aware of it all the time. There had been the obvious signs indicated by Claire's frequent absences explained away by work, short temper and worse, the excuses for not making love. To lose Claire was like being deprived of the other self that she wasn't but would like to be—outgoing, aggressive, strong. All of these qualities were stored in an attractive, always stylishly groomed Claire with an open face that inevitably enticed friends. Where had *she* failed? In her droll dependent sameness? Like flatness beneath a mountain.

The class bell pealed throughout the building. Three o'clock. Her Shakespeare class met—the last one for today. She put out the cigarette in the Oglethorpe ashtray and gathered up her notes to go to the only place where she felt self-assured—the classroom.

II

In the evening when she arrived home, Frizzle greeted her happily, jumping up and down, barking out his excitement. Penelope bent down to pat him, holding his furry body close to her, feeling his warmth, another heart. To her, it was so different now. With Claire, there had been life: people, music, gaiety. When Claire left, the blithe people followed her.

Penelope straightened up, taking off her coat and throwing it carelessly on the couch which was already laden with books and newspapers. The ash trays on the coffee table were powdered with dead ashes, and a half cup of coffee still remained from the morning. Untidyness didn't matter anymore. Why should it, when no one came.

Sighing wearily, she automatically began her routine of turning on the TV. A handsome male newscaster entered the room on the screen, providing sound, stimulating company. Next in succession came the dinner preparation. Another chore that once was fun: cooking favorite recipes for Claire. They would sit across from each other in the dining room and eat like Epicureans with candles embellishing the meal. Claire would talk spiritedly about her day: the customers, shop, incidents while she sat quietly sipping the dinner wine and taking on a new, more exhilarating life vicariously through Claire.

She opened the refrigerator. It was practically empty. Two eggs, a half

quart of milk, and a wilted head of lettuce were on the shelves. Impossible.
She couldn't go to the store. Not tonight. Tomorrow she would be more
prepared to withstand the clamour of the glittering huge supermarket,
commanding herself to push the cart down the aisles and pick up more
than she needed so that she would not have to go back for a long while.
Searching in the cabinets, she found a can of tomato soup. She would
open it. Frizzle had enough food. In accordance with her unvarying pattern, she ate, worked on another chapter, and went to bed.

III

With the passing of weeks, Penelope discovered that J. D. was an excellent
worker. She reported to the office regularly and on time, flopping down
in the rickety chair at the table. Seated there, she would bend slightly
over the typewriter, spreading her full muscular jean-clad thighs.

Watching her one afternoon, Penelope broke her usual tacit reserve to
remark: "You type well," conceding that some praise should be given for
motivation and appreciation.

"Been doing it long enough—" the girl murmured, not interrupting her
steady typing pace.

"What are you going to do when you graduate?" Penelope probed
curiously.

"Work my way through grad school, I guess."

Penelope focused her eyes on the back of J. D.'s neck where the
close-cropped blonde hair sloped down straight in coarse singular straw
strands. Claire's hair was dark and curly, flecked with gray. J. D. paused
to stretch, throwing her arms high above her head like weight lifter.
Penelope noticed the movement of her broad shoulders. Like a prowler,
the thought sneaked into her mind of how the girl's back would feel
lined against the palms of her hands—flesh touching flesh, skin touching
warmth. It had been so long.

"That all for today, Dr. Bullock?" J. D. had suddenly turned around
and was looking at her.

Penelope flinched, angry at her thoughts, and at the girl who had
caught her off guard. Anxiety pricked her. Had her mind's picture been
mirrored in her face?

"Yes, Miss Downs, that will be all for today," she said curtly, feigning
absorption in the papers on her desk.

"Wow! Look at that!" J. D. exclaimed, pointing out the window.

Penelope turned to see the white flakes emptying from the sky. February
had to have its show. All seasons bear their raiment. "It's really coming
down, isn't it?" Penelope observed. "I guess I had better get on the high-

way before it gets too bad."

"You don't live on campus?"

"No—in town."

J. D. put the cover on the typewriter and got her coat from the rack by the door. "Drive carefully, Dr. Bullock," she advised, before leaving.

"I will—" Penelope replied, a little astonished that someone should care.

She drove slowly, cautiously, and at the edge of the campus, recognized J. D. standing at the bus stop, a lone figure dusted with flakes of snow. Penelope stopped the car and rolled down the window on the passenger's side. "Can I give you a lift somewhere?"

"You sure can!" J. D. smiled appreciatively, stomping her feet free of the white flakes before getting in. "I live in town too. I think I've missed the bus."

"It's really coming down," Penelope said worriedly, peering through a snow-crusted windshield which the wiper wasn't coping with effectively.

"You got snow tires?" J. D. questioned anxiously.

Penelope nodded. "Perhpas it isn't as bad in the direction we're going." Maybe she should have gotten a room in the faculty clubhouse for the night. But there was Frizzle to be fed and let out. This was the first time she had been caught alone driving in a snowstorm. Claire was usually with her and Claire drove.

"Can you see ok, Dr. Bullock? I can drive pretty good. I used to hustle a bootleg cab."

Penelope laughed. "What is it you *haven't* done, Miss Downs?" Suddenly the car skidded as she maneuvered to enter the icy patch of the ramp to the expressway. Panicking, she inadvertently jammed on the brakes and the car turned in a half arc. "Whew!"

"Let *me* drive," J. D. said quickly, sounding out a hidden order.

Shaken, Penelope moved over. J. D. got out and went around to the driver's side. "We'll make it," she said confidently, face determined, starting the car. "Don't worry. I *like* challenges."

Penelope huddled rigidly in the corner, chastising herself for her weakness, obeisance to the girl's dominance. Imagine! A grown woman permitting a girl to take charge, handle her like an idiot too stupid to cope with what was a simple matter of driving skill. Why had she done it? Out of habit—a nagging ghost of Claire?

J. D. drove as expertly as she typed. The snow was tapering off and in this relief, she forgot her cardinal dogma and reached in her purse for a cigarette.

"May I have one too?" J. D. asked, eyes ahead on the road.

"Certainly—" There was no other answer she could give.

J. D. pushed in the lighter and held it to Penelope's cigarette before lighting her own. "You can relax now, Dr. Bullock," she said, squinting over the smoke from the cigarette limp in the corner of her mouth. "We're almost there."

The city's lights, dimmed by the falling snow, shone like filmy globes in the evening's limpid coating of dusk.

IV

The girl had insisted on driving her all the way home. At the apartment, Penelope invited her in. "Won't you have dinner with me?"

"I don't want to be a bother," J. D. said, hesitating.

"Nonsense, I *want* you to." It was true. She wanted to prolong the company of her. It would be a change to have someone to talk with and prepare for. Moreover, she owed it to her.

"All right—"

Inside, Frizzle immediately fell in love with J. D. They cavorted together on the floor and J. D. played with him like a child. Looking down at them, Penelope asked teasingly: "Are you of the drinking age? I have some brandy." Brandy was safe and refined to offer a student coming in out of the cold.

"I'd rather have bourbon, if you got it," J. D. said sheepishly. "And, I've been drinking since I was sixteen."

"How many years ago was that?" Penelope called back, going into the kitchen, amusement in her tone.

"Seven!"

When Penelope returned to the living room with a tray of bourbon, ice and glasses, J. D. was seated on the couch watching TV. Her firm thick thighs were spread wide in her usual way with her feet, encased in brown suede laced bootshoes damp from the snow, planted firmly on the floor.

"Here you are—" Penelope said, setting the tray on the coffee table. "Help yourself. You deserve it." Was it her imagination or did the girl's eyes brush her breasts. "I'll have dinner ready soon—" Flushing, she moved hastily away.

While eating, Penelope thought it was nice having someone seated across from her at the table again. Even Frizzle seemed contented, curled between them. J. D. ate with the unabashedness of youth when hungry, passing her plate for seconds of the lamb chops and peas. Afterwards, she helped Penelope wash the dishes, commenting that she had been a dishwasher also at one time.

The evening went too swiftly for Penelope and when she heard J. D. say that she had to go, a forlorn feeling invaded her. "I'm not rushing you—"

"The gang's probably wondering about me. I share an apartment with two others—a student nurse and a sometime artist. Plus, we have two dogs and a cat. It gets kind of crowded sometimes," she smiled in a way that revealed she really didn't mind. And as an afterthought: "Dr. Bullock, may I come to work tomorrow in the afternoon instead of morning? I'd like to stay in bed longer."

"What?" Penelope was distracted, trying to envision an apartment filled with three people, two dogs and a cat.

"Work—tomorrow. In the afternoon—"

"Yes. Make it around four o'clock, after my last class."

"Thanks for everything, Dr. Bullock—" J. D. said; eyes grateful upon her.

"It's rather late to be standing on a corner waiting for a bus. You're welcome to spend the night. I have an extra room—" she hastened to inform her, an addendum she felt was needed.

"Nope, I can make it all right. I'm used to it."

Looking at J. D. buttoning up her coat and pulling the triangular cap down firmly over her ears, Penelope felt she could make it anywhere. "I'll see you tomorrow."

"I'll be there—" J. D. promised.

Penelope turned off the lights in the living room and went to the window. There she opened the curtain to watch J. D. walk in her bear-like wide-legged lope down the street to the bus stop. Loneliness flooded her like the bone-chilling spectre of the damned.

V

It was a brisk windy first day of March, and for some reason, the sound of J. D.'s typewriter irritated Penelope. The steady clicking of the keys and snapping back and forth of the carriage slammed against her ears like a freight train. Head down over the papers, she furtively watched the girl out of the corners of her eyes. Ever since that snowy evening when they had dinner together, J. D.'s presence in the closeness of the office unnerved her. Frequently she would find herself gazing absently at the side of the girl's face, scrutinizing the slightly broad nose which now had an angry red pimple on the corner, and at the rippling motions of the broad shoulders in the white open-necked shirt. Most of all, her eyes lingered on the thick, short fingers as they pounded the keys. Fingers were important for fingers could produce body warmth, body music in tune with the heart.

"Something wrong, Dr. Bullock?"

Penelope startled, pretending to rustle the papers before her. "I beg your pardon?"

"You've been so quiet lately. I just wondered if you're ok."

"Yes—I'm fine. Perhaps working too hard."

J. D. faced her, half scissoring one jean leg over her thigh. "All work— no play. What do you do for relaxation?"

Penelope stiffened. How dare she! A student prying into her private life. The answer was frigid: "I read—go to the theatre—"

"Don't you have a friend?" The girl's blue eyes swallowed her.

"A friend?" She echoed the word which made a hollow sound in her ears.

"Yeah—you know. Somebody to go places and *do* things with."

"Of course!" she snapped back too quickly, agitated by the excessively personal connotation of the conversation. Once more disregarding her rule, Penelope sought for the pack of cigarettes hidden in her drawer.

"Me too?" J. D. asked softly, coming over to her.

Penelope handed her the pack along with a book of matches. The striking of the match sounded sharply in the jelled stillness. Passing the cigarettes and matches back, J. D.'s fingers brushed hers. The contact, light as a breath, stayed heavy on her skin. Her hand shook when lighting her cigarette.

"You're all tight inside," J. D. said gently, blowing out a smoke veil between them. "Look outside. The sun's shining for a change and the air's crisp and good. Want to go for a ride? I'll drive. You can sit back and relax."

Penelope saw that the sun *was* shining, a pale gold in the cool belly of the sky. The winter had been long, dreary, tiresome, molded in gray, clay days. "You've persuaded me," she laughed, amazed at her response.

"You're pretty when you laugh."

"What am I when I don't?" Penelope parried defensively.

"You're still pretty. Only laughter erases something." J. D.'s fingers stretched out to touch the narrow creased path between Penelope's eyes. "You frown too much. You're getting permanent lines there—"

"Age. I'm getting permanent lines everywhere—" Penelope said, trying to make her voice light. Why was youth so unknowingly vicious. Methodically she twisted out the cigarette, observing the lines in her hand too. Claire had noted that you can tell a woman's age by her neck and hands.

"You're not *that* old—" J. D. protested tactfully.

"Compared to *you*, my dear, I'm ancient."

"Age is irrelevant. It's how people react to each other that matters. You know, being together and liking the same things." Her voice lowered. "I think *we* have a lot in common."

Penelope realized the dialogue at this point needed stopping. She got her coat. "We'd better go for that ride before I change my mind and give you more work to do." This was the time to draw the line between student and teacher. She had come from a family of academicians. A father who had chaired the history department at Northwestern, and a mother who had taught languages. Students were those to teach, chat with over tea and coffee, but never to withdraw the formalities in company with. She had been indoctrinated in her parents' delineation of student and faculty relationships by sight and sound in their neat faculty house.

J. D. ground out her cigarette in the Oglethorpe ashtray, leaving the tell-tale social marks of two: Penelope's rimmed with faint lipstick, and J. D.'s without. "Let's go—" She threw on her denim jacket, and grinning, held the door open for Penelope. The gesture made Penelope wonder if this was deference to age, respect, or—

She had difficulty keeping up with J. D.'s long, quick strides to the parking lot. J. D. was shorter than she, head level to her shoulders. Walking with J. D. gave her mixed feelings. She supposed they looked like what they were: faculty and student. J. D.'s jacket was open exposing the gray and red Oglethorpe sweat shirt. Penelope thought: *If I had had a daughter at the age of nineteen—*

"Smell the air!" J. D. breathed ecstatically, head flung back, inhaling deeply. "I like to go walking in the woods just to breathe the air. Don't you?"

"I've never walked in the woods—" Penelope confessed. Claire wasn't the outdoors type and neither was she. Claire liked the indoor things of life—the theatre, parties, dinners.

"When it gets warmer, we'll go," J. D. said, as if it were understood.

Just like that! What made the girl so presumptuous, taking over. Treating her like an equal. When they came to the car, Penelope handed J. D. the keys.

On the highway, they rode in silence, until J. D. turned on the radio. A young woman's voice joined them, singing a sad nostalgic song about love. "That's a local singer," J. D. identified. Then offhandedly: "She's gay."

A warning fear suddenly enmeshed Penelope, fastening her tightly within. Make no comment, she cautioned herself. Forget the girl's words, pretend she hadn't heard. She stared fixedly at the straight hard stretch of highway. Cars passed them, leaving noisy sounds behind. Scattered farmhouses, sentry telephone poles, and budding green fields flanked them on each side.

Like an accusing ghost, the word J. D. had spoken so casually returned, stained with guilt—gay. She and Claire had studiously avoided the word in their early days together. They did not wish to face it. *They* were not gay—the others were. For themselves, they had no specific label or name

for what they were: two women in love living like a married couple.
After Claire joined a consciousness-raising group, she began to use the
word quite freely. Penelope had refused to follow her to the sessions that
to her were nothing but women trying to act as lay psychologists. Basically,
she knew the real reason why she shunned the group was because of her
shyness. She regretted afterwards that she hadn't gone, for that was where
Claire had met Rosalyn who took her away.

"You have any gay friends?" J. D. asked abruptly.

Penelope's fingers curled and uncurled on her lap. Watch it. Control
was what she needed. "If they are, I don't know it," she replied stiffly,
thinking it was a good, safe, evasive answer.

"Strange. Everybody's coming out these days. Even *me!*" J. D. laughed.
"What's there to be ashamed of?"

What indeed? But there is that to be *afraid* of. "Do you usually
announce your sex preference to everybody?" Penelope questioned
frostily, upset because the girl had confided in her. She wished that she
hadn't, for she did not want to know, to be laden with this private
knowledge that would make her more wary, instill an extra caution into
their relationship.

"If they want to know or I want to tell them, why not?" J. D. retorted.

Penelope reflected on her answer. The courage of youth who have
nothing to lose, who do not consider the future, only the present and
importance of it to them. The establishment was the old, however; someday, they would be a part of it, the structure that made and held fast to
the rules. What would it be then? Change the subject. Do not become
didactic. Penelope began an inane conversation about a recent best seller
she had read. The topic was harmless. She was again in control.

Farther down the road, they saw a sign advertising food and drinks.
"Are you hungry?" J. D. asked, slowing down. "There's a place—"

"All right. Stop if you wish." The restaurant was L-shaped with a
stone facade. It was practically empty except for two middle-aged men
in khaki pants and cotton shirts lounging over a quart of beer. As they
went in, the men turned their heads in unison to appraise them, as men
automatically do with women. The one with the thinning blonde hair
made a remark at which the second man sniggered.

Penelope was made conscious of the contrast in their attire: J. D.
with her faded jeans and windbreaker, and she in a rust colored polyester
dress and matching spring coat. J. D. moved ahead of her, walking in her
self-assured swagger to stop at a table near the front. "This ok?"

"Yes—"

A waitress appeared, quickly putting water and place settings before
them. Penelope looked at the plastic mats with the picture of the restau-

rant on it which was named The Hideaway. "I'll just have a cup of black coffee—" she said, not accustomed to eating this time of day.

"Well, *I'm* hungry! I'm going to have a hamburger with onions, french fries and a bottle of beer." Looking over at Penelope, she smiled. "You won't mind my onion breath, will you?"

"Why should I?" Besides, onion decisions were for lovers.

When the waitress left, J. D. slouched back in the chair, hooking her thumbs under her belt and said: "I like you."

Penelope felt unnerved at the candidness of the girl. How did she mean it? As a person? To give herself time for forming a reply, she busied herself with taking off her coat and folding it neatly on the empty chair beside her. "Thank you, Miss Downs. I'm pleased when my students like me. Many look askance at their professors."

"Why don't you ask me *why* I like you?" the girl continued, seemingly amused in her probing, lips curled downwards.

A precautionary signal sirened within Penelope. Be careful. The girl admittedly was gay. Don't let the situation get out of hand. Put up your protective barriers. She couldn't afford to come out like others of her colleagues. To catch harassment from the administration. Oglethorpe was still a conservative, private institution ruled by those who were determined to keep it that way. Don't get trapped.

"It really doesn't matter *why* you like me, Miss Downs. It's just nice to know that you do."

"Yes, it does," J. D. persisted doggedly. "The *reason* why people like each other is *important*. I like you because underneath your cool and formal exterior, I can see a very different person—congenial, warm. The person I'd like to *reach*. The only thing is you won't let yourself go. Relax. You always look as if you're afraid somebody's going to find out something about you that you want to keep hidden."

Penelope reached for the glass of water. A necessary gesture to moisten the dryness in her throat. The water was warm and tasted of fluoride. "Do I? Like skeletons in my closet?" *Closet!* The wrong word. What was it? Claire had flung at her: *Get out of the closet.*

"Yeah—something like that." The girl's face was a void.

The waitress brought their order. "Anything else?"

Penelope noticed she was young, pretty and a natural blonde. They didn't even want middle-aged waitresses anymore. Everything must be surrounded with youth. She shook her head.

J. D. ate hungrily, covering the french fries with layers of catsup. Penelope concentrated on the hands clutching the sandwich, fingers strong, nails closely clipped and cuticles meticulously pushed back to show half-moons. Claire's fingers were long, slender, delicate with natural

painted nails to duplicate her lipstick. Everything had to match with
Claire, shoes, purse, hat—people. Apparently Rosalyn was more analogous
to Claire than she.

The coffee had a leftover too strong taste. She pushed it away. J. D.
drank her beer thirstily. "You should have ordered a drink." She signaled
the waitress. "Scotch and soda."

Penelope's mouth tightened disapprovingly. The *nerve* of her! When
the waitress left, the words came out in a tumultuous gust: "What made
you think that *I* wanted a drink?"

"Intuition—" J. D. smiled, unruffled by the anger. "Woman to woman
intuition."

"*You* are not *exactly* a *woman* to me—"

Pain reddened J. D.'s face as her eyes showed hurt. "What do you
mean? Just because I told you I was gay, I'm not a *woman* to you?"

"No—no. I meant in terms of maturity—" Penelope explained swiftly,
wanting to erase the hurt as rapidly as she had drawn it.

"Oh?" J. D. frowned, looking at her quietly, perceptively. "I can give
you a few pointers on *that* too! I'll bet I've had more worldly experience
than you've ever had."

The talk was severed by the waitress bringing her drink. Penelope
reached for it hurriedly, needing its sustenance to maintain her equilibrium.
The drink went down better than the coffee, stirring currents of warmth.

Sensing the effect, J. D. looked satisfied. "See, I knew that was what
you needed. When you're out to relax—*relax*. That's my motto."

"Yes—teacher," Penelope jested.

"Everybody can learn something from somebody else."

"Homespun philosophy—"

"Voice of experience," J. D. retorted, forking up the last of her
potatoes.

When Penelope finished her drink, it was like losing a crutch. "I think
I'll have another."

"And I'm going to have another beer." J. D. pushed her well cleaned
plate away. A smudge of catsup made paint on her chin. The onion smell
still lingered, sharp and pungent.

They savored the second round slowly. Penelope tried to remember
the last time she had done this—with anybody. The waitress came with
the check and Penelope opened her purse.

"Nope—" J. D. stopped her. "This is on me. After all, it was *my* idea.
To help you relax."

Penelope did not insist, even though she thought of the money and
J. D.'s financial standing as a student. Allow her her pride.

"You can do it next time—" J. D. winked.

Next time! The effrontery of her. Who said that there would be a next time. Hastily she put on her coat. "We had better go. I have some more work to do on my book," she stated evenly, reverting to her role. As they passed the table with the two men, one stared hard at J. D. and muttered to his companion: *"Dyke!"*

The label slid like the edge of a knife's blade in Penelope's ears. But J. D. laughed loudly, throwing her head back in a challengingly proud way, looking back at the man. With great ceremony, she held the door open for Penelope. Fresh air blew against her like a savior.

VI

The loneliness persisted like incessant rain. She waited two weeks before succumbing to inviting J. D. over again. It was a dinner invitation shielded by the explanation that there was some important work she had to get out in a hurry and she didn't want to stay in her office at night to do it. The work was simply an article that was overdue for a professional journal.

J. D. came over and typed with the same vigor as she had devoured the hamburger dinner. By eleven o'clock, she had finished. "You really worked me tonight," she said, yawning tiredly.

"I'm sorry, but this was something I had simply been procrastinating about. It is late. Why don't you spend the night? I can fix the bed in the guest room." Without waiting for her reply, Penelope went into the room she and Claire had used for a subterfuge when parents, relatives and straight friends visited. This was until Claire, coming home from one of her consciousness-raising sessions, scowled in disgust: "To hell with this shit. I sleep with you and that's that. If people don't like it, they needn't waste time to come by."

"Who's that?" J. D. had followed her and was pointing at a picture of Claire on the dresser.

"A friend—" A neutral word. Also a word that could carry an innuendo. She reached in the closet for linen.

"She's attractive—" J. D. said pensively. "I told you everybody should have a friend."

Claire's face smiled back at them. Claire didn't show her age as much as she. Claire's youth was kept alive by her fervent joie de vivre. J. D. had a drink in her hand which she stirred with her finger. "Do you get lonely living here by yourself?"

"Lonely? No—I *like* living alone." The lie turned inside of her and screamed. She missed Claire. Hastily, she made a production of dipping pillows into pockets of yellow pillowcases the same color as the sheets.

Claire liked to sleep on colored linen. "Makes it sexier—" she used to laugh. She missed the close feel of Claire's body at night, the two of them folding into each other like an accordion. A familiar twitch throbbed between her legs like a sweet ache.

Turning to J. D., she said: "Your bed's all prepared."

"I'm not ready to go to bed yet."

Penelope shrugged. "Go when you choose. I'm ready."

"Aren't you going to have a drink with me before you do?" J. D.'s face was as open as a child's, appealing.

"No, I think not. I'm really not too much for drinking."

J. D. looked at her closely over the glass. "You're not too much for anything, are you?"

Frizzle came in wagging his tail. Penelope bent to pat him, getting out of the range of J. D.'s piercing stare. Suddenly contrition flooded her. The girl had worked hard, and she really could have refused to come over at night to do it. She should at least show her gratitude. "All right—" she said softly, facing her. "I'll have a nightcap with you."

"I'll get it. I like to fix drinks."

Penelope sat on the couch in the living room, nursing the overly strong scotch and soda while watching J. D. sprawled on the floor going through her records. Penelope realized the collection was not all to J. D.'s taste— classics mostly. Claire had taken her part—jazz, pops, show tunes.

"No Jill Hill's—" J. D. said disappointedly.

"Sorry—" She sipped on the drink. Claire used to try to get her to loosen up over a drink. *You're so damn priggish at times.*

"Do you have many male friends?" J. D. questioned unexpectedly.

Penelope stiffened, hands squeezing around her glass. "Why?" she fired back, uncontrollably defensive.

"I don't see any pictures around and I've never seen you with any on campus in a *friendly* way—" she added, smiling slightly.

"I have a few—" The second lie for the evening was garbled in swallowing her drink. The girl shouldn't be prying into her private life. This dissolved the teacher-pupil relationship.

J. D. stacked the records back into the cabinet. "I had a couple of boyfriends once. Even went to bed with one. Ugh!"

Penelope brightened at this admission. Now was the opportunity to detract. The cliché came readily to her lips, for what lesbian at some time or another hadn't heard it: "You'll find the right man someday."

"I'm not *looking* for a man!" J. D. shouted back emphatically, eyes narrowing. "Are you?"

"I really don't have time for a man in my life—at this point," Penelope replied airily, believing it best to place the talk on a lighter plane. Too much seriousness breeds deepness.

"*Everybody* has some time for what they want—if they *want* it."

Penelope set her glass down abruptly. "I'm going to bed. You do whatever you like. There're cold cuts, beer and cheese in the refrigerator. See you in the morning—" She smiled a polite goodnight. Get away. Fast. Hurry.

"Thanks. Pleasant dreams—" J. D.'s lips curled in a derisive smirk as Penelope almost fled out of the room.

VII

She finally went to sleep on the thumping sounds of a rock station that J. D. had turned on in the living room. The music blasted through the closed door and protective walls like a hounding monster. It seemed as if she had been asleep only a short time before she felt J. D. shaking her and calling her name. J. D. had switched on the bedlamp and was standing beside the bed clad only in her underwear. Her body showed thick and white, the ample breasts spilling half out of a pink brassiere, stomach bulging over flowered bikini briefs where the light hairs of her pubic area sprouted from the edges like fine pieces of straw.

"I want to sleep with you," J. D. announced poutingly.

The surprise awakening and words caught Penelope off guard. Her eyes widened, glowing at the half naked girl beside her. Penelope's mouth arched in a grim reproving line. "I prepared a bed for you—"

"I prepared a bed for you," J. D. mimicked in a prim falsetto. Defiantly she sat down on the edge of the bed. "I *said* that I want to sleep in here with *you.*" Pulling the covers back, she crawled inside and lay her head in a small dent in the pillow where Penelope's head had been.

Penelope stiffened as the girl's smooth body touched hers. She could see the speckles of brown freckles on her face and smell the mixture of bourbon and cigarette smoke on her breath. A faint odor of perspiration emanated from the heat in her body—heat that suffused out and warmed her like a flame. There was another in bed with her where a body had not been for a long time. Here something was being offered to her— something in the human relationship of giving and taking in the guise of the flesh. She trembled—remembering. Their eyes met: the girl's challenging the woman's. What J. D. saw made her laugh softly, knowingly, before she ventured to move over the restricted border and kiss Penelope gently on the mouth.

J. D.'s mouth was thin and small, and to Penelope's amazement, she kissed shyly. Suddenly Penelope gave a small stifled cry and half rose above her, pressing her lips harder against the girl's, opening her mouth and groaning into it with released longing. The flowing lava of need spread throughout her loins, making her a strong forceful Amazon, bending the girl at will. Confidently, her hands sought to undo the brassiere. She wanted to feel the pendulous globes, to knead, bite and kiss them, to bury her face between the vales of them. J. D. gasped out her pleasure, eyes closed, arms clasped about her. Penelope became the aggressor, tactful, knowledgeable, sure as the lover. She removed the briefs and felt the telltale moisture below. She marveled at it, astonished that she, Penelope Bullock, could make someone feel, want, desire—*her*. She had power. She was the provocator. The girl held to her expectantly, submissively, breathing hard.

Penelope outlined their bodies together and began to move slowly, very slowly, closing her eyes. The strange new strength of her ebbed through her, alarming her, making her aware of what she could do—*be* to somebody else. The girl was making moaning sounds, body trembling, squeezing her hard, and Penelope grasped her tighter, becoming what she had never been before, a tigress in her newly found self.

VIII

The morning came quickly, brutal in its harsh light's judgment. Penelope awakened to find herself alone in the bed. Sounds and smells from the kitchen located J. D. for her. She lay still, needing the time alone to reflect on herself. Claire had always been the aggressor. But the union of youth and age had reversed her role. Behind J. D.'s outward braggadocio was a hidden diffidence. This was brought out in bed. What J. D. lacked in experience was made up for by her youthful, passionate enthusiasm and quickness to respond.

Why did the girl want to go to bed with her? Her body was too thin and marred by a surgical scar. Her breasts were beginning to sag and the pubic hair was specked with gray. Guilt clouded her thoughts. How could she have been so weak? To make love to a girl—a student. Human physical weakness stronger than the mind. Male professors made love to their female students. She had heard them laugh about "trading a grade for a piece." She had thought it outrageous. Now here she was having her sexual desires gratified by a student. But J. D. had made the approach and there was not a bargain involved. What did the girl want—if anything?

"Breakfast!" J. D. called cheerfully, entering the room with a tray. "See—I can cook too!"

Penelope took in her youthful freshness in the jeans and shirt. Outside morning traffic sounds made her conscious of others beyond their world "Thank you."

"Bacon, eggs, toast and coffee," J. D. itemized, placing the tray in front of her. "I want to watch you eat." She perched at the foot of the bed.

Penelope sat up, pulling the covers higher, mindful of her nudity. She ate sparingly, not hungry, embarrassed by the girl watching her. Thoughts nagged her like a predator until the girl leaned forward to stop them with a kiss.

"You're so quiet," J. D. whispered in her ear. "Are you sorry about last night? I thought it was fantastic. You're a beautiful lover—"

Penelope set the tray aside on the nighttable and got up. Age makes an experienced lover. A cool draft enveloped her body. She looked down at her gown, crumpled on the floor where she had flung it. Now it appeared obscene. Shakily, she picked it up, hastily covering herself.

"Why do you want it on?" J. D. questioned. "I think it's real sexy to walk around bare-assed."

Sexy. Claire walked around naked all the time. Claire had taught her about sex and sexiness. "I'm going to take a bath."

In a few minutes, J. D. followed her into the bathroom. "Let's take a bath together."

Penelope stopped brushing her teeth. "Oh, J. D.!" she cried in exasperation. The bathroom was her private domain. In it, she performed all the secret body functions of toilet: cleaning her partial, putting in her contact lenses, taking a douche, and shaving the hairs on her legs and under her arms.

The touch of J. D.'s lips on the back of her neck made her shiver. A resurging of last night crawled an annoying ache in her groin. Once the fire had been awakened—

"Please—Penny—let's do it together—"

The shocking intimacy of the name. No one, ever, had called her Penny. Not her parents—nor Claire.

They did it together, soaping, sponging, laughing with the warm sudsy water sensuous against them. J. D. stopped her merriment for a moment when Penelope's hand brushed her breast. Then she asked: "You ever done it in a bath tub?"

In reply, Penelope said huskily: "No. Let's—"

"Crazy!" J. D. whooped as Penelope's body neared hers under the perfumed cover of the water.

IX

The days had a new dimension for Penelope with J. D. sparking life into them—her. On weekends, J. D. came over and they talked. J. D.'s talk was about her roommates, the animal menagerie, and gay friends.

Penelope listened half in amusement, half in tolerance, offering comments and oftentimes sage advice. She was only too glad to have even this talk bouncing against walls that had become a tomb. J. D.'s gossip and inane chitchat was unlike what she and Claire had shared. After all, their exchanges were shaped by the same age, experiences and interests. J. D.'s parley was light and refreshing, leaving nothing ponderous to reflect upon. The physical part made up for the shallowness of verbal communication. This was exciting and wild, unlike the sophistication with Claire.

In her office, Penelope tried to maintain an aloof, impersonal dignity with J. D. Sometimes it worked, sometimes it didn't. At the times when desire was transmitted by a touch, look or memory, they would automatically move into each other's arms, Penelope embracing the short, squat body of J. D., rubbing her hands over the broad back and on down to cup the large buttocks into her. On occasions, in the cubicle office, they made love standing up against the wall, in a chair, and on the edge of the desk. The lovemaking was hurried, for there was always the fear that someone would knock. The furtiveness of it excited them more, with the heat strong between them, painful and vicious.

Students and faculty members began to comment on how alive and well Penelope was looking. She walked more briskly now, smiled more, and bloomed like a woman being treated well by love. She was an autumn flower in blossom.

The incriminating fears of the effects of a faculty and student affair were all pushed aside. The weekends abolished doubts. She looked forward eagerly to them and being with J. D. The apartment became a different place and each room had a distinctive connotation. They made variant love in all of them. Penelope was amazed by how easily kisses and caresses came to her. How she could lose herself in another. She forgot how unattractive she thought she was, for in love and loving, she became beautiful to herself.

By April, the month of transition when spring flowers are blessed by the gentle wetness of rain, a warm, heady balminess filled the air. Penelope began to notice a restlessness in J. D. She came over less frequently, blaming it on preparing for finals. After all, she was graduating in June. Besides, she was busy writing letters and filling out applications for grad school. She wanted to go to Columbia. Upon hearing this, Penelope felt threatened by the unknown. J. D. would be gone. New York was far away. The future was uncertain. Thoughts became upsetting. Her familiar pattern was tearing apart at the seams like an old dress. Consistency was her life's mainstay.

One late May evening, J. D. moved more restively than usual around the apartment. She switched radio dials, TV channels, drank beer, pro-

gressed to wine, and finally put out the half smoked cigarette to take
out a joint which she said was really what she wanted in the first place.
Lying on the floor, she leisurely nursed the weed while gazing up reflectively at the ceiling. Penelope tried to suppress her irritation by working
on her book. From time to time, she glanced fretfully at her, signaling
her distaste at the habit J. D. had recently brought out before her.

Finishing her self-indulgence, J. D. got up slowly from the floor, a
vacant smile on her face. "Let's go someplace. I'm tired of sitting around
here doing nothing."

Penelope looked up from her work. The facts *were* that young people
were restless, got bored easily, and liked to be on the move. "Anyplace
in mind?" she asked stiffly.

"Just someplace for a drink."

"There's plenty to drink here—" Penelope hastened to point out.
Actually, all she wanted to do was stay here and write.

"Yeah, but it's not like going *out* for a drink where there's music and
people."

Penelope turned from her desk with a sigh. "All right," she acquiesced.
"Let's go."

They went to a bar J. D. liked that catered to both gay and straight
on an off-street uptown. J. D. drank wine and Penelope dawdled over a
weak scotch and soda. J. D. looked spaced out, face flushed, hair falling
in disarray over her forehead. The loud music from a long-haired group
of five, among whose players Penelope couldn't distinguish the males from
females, slammed like bricks over the room, cast out by two guitars, a
saxophone, piano and drum.

J. D. kept her eyes on the group, snapping her fingers and gyrating in
the chair as if her rear end were on fire. From time to time, she would
emit a "yeah—yeah—yeah" to the beat. Penelope sipped the drink, hoping
they wouldn't have to stay long. She begrudged the time away from her
writing. J. D. turned to say something to her and stopped as her eyes
focused on two girls entering the room. The one walking in front had
long red hair falling around a pale baby face enhanced with artificial
eyelashes shielding blue mascara'd eyes. She wore a cowgirl outfit con-
sisting of black shiny boots to her knees, a black leather skirt and vest,
red shirt, black string tie, and a black cowgirl hat. Her companion, tall
and slim with hard eyes, wore blue slacks and a white shirt opened wide
at the neck.

The cowgirl was apparently popular, for little squeals of delight from
females went up instantly at her entrance. Smiling, obviously pleased,
she paused and talked with those calling to her. When she reached Penelope
and J. D., she stopped, a look of surprise on her face.

"J. D.! *Where* have you been hiding?" she asked, flinging her hair
back like a mane.

"J. D.'s eyelids lowered in the manner Penelope had learned was shy
pleasure. "Been trying to get through college. I *told* you I'd make it
someday."

The girl giggled a tinkle of amusement. "You sure did. Congratulations!"
There was a fleeting look of admiration on her face. Then noticing
Penelope, she said: "Is this your mother?"

Penelope felt the stab in the pit of her stomach as her breath drew
in sharply. "Do we *look* alike?" she interrupted coldly, furious.

"This is a friend of mine—" J. D. threw in quickly, offering nothing
more.

"Oh? How interesting—" the girl sniggered meaningfully, eyes disdainful
on Penelope. Turning back to J. D., she said softly: "I've missed you."

The second girl who had come in with her emerged out of the shadows.
"Come on," she said impatiently, "Sealy's waiting for us at her table."

"Call me sometime—" the cowgirl waved back, led away by her
companion.

For a long while, J. D. sat broodingly silent, running her finger up
and down the wine glass. Finally she announced: "I'm going to the john."
She got up waveringly, disappearing in the nebulous direction in which
the cowgirl had gone.

Left alone, Penelope found the music a monotonous cataclysmic sound,
splitting her ears. A few were initiating a dance to its sounds, far apart,
each in her own subjective motion, oblivious to the other, companions
only in the music. She and Claire used to dance close together. Nostalgia
comes solely with age. She needed another drink. The waitress came over
at her signal.

"I'd like another—" she ordered. Then, because she had to, she asked:
"Do you know the girl in the cowgirl outfit?" Did it matter? Of course
it did. All things and persons connected with J. D. mattered.

The waitress shifted her gum before responding. She, like the others
in the place, was young. "Sure—" she said brightly, "that's Jill Hill. She
used to sing in here before she started on the way up in big time. Didn't
J. D. tell you?" The waitress leaned over confidentially, and Penelope
could see a pink brassiere strap skirting her shoulder like a bandtape.
"She and J. D. used to be lovers."

Penelope looked across the room to see Jill Hill coming out of the
john to sit down at a table of admirers—all young, excited, impressionable,
vivacious, eager to ambush. At the edge of the bar, she saw a woman her
age with too-bright yellow hair swooping over a worn face, tense, smoking
and drinking beer, trying not to seem too alone—too lonely—out of place.

"Here you are—" the waitress brought her drink.

"May I have the check?" All at once she did not want the drink. The place was strangling her like a shrieking accusing prophet. Shakily she paid and left without a backward glance at the direction J. D. had disappeared.

X

Penelope's phone rang far into the night, stalking her. Eventually she stopped its hunt by taking the receiver off the hook. The next day, she stayed home from work, something she rarely did, pleading illness. For a week, she stayed in, refusing to answer J. D.'s knocks or phone calls. To offset these, she plunged feverishly into her writing, losing herself in the book. Milton was her redeemer.

When she did return to work, J. D. was there in the office working. Upon seeing Penelope, puzzlement crossed her face to merge with youthful innocence. "What did I do wrong?"

"Nothing—" Penelope looked away from her. "It just had to end." As in La Fontaine's *The Fox and the Gnat:* "In everything one must consider the end." It was best to do it now before it went too long and the hurt would be deeper.

"Why?"

Penelope sat down at her desk, recalling this was where she sat when J. D. first walked in. "It couldn't work—" And it was ending anyhow.

J. D. moved to sit on the desk. "You *liked* me—everything."

"Yes." Why pretend? She liked good food, books, and wine too.

"It's over, hon?"

"We can still remain friends. If I can help you in any way—" Penelope offered stiltedly. She and Claire had not remained friends or even acquaintances. Can ex-lovers ever really become friends without remembering the loving and how it used to be?

"This is the last day to work for you according to my work contract. I wanted to finish everything," J. D. told her, getting up from the desk.

"I know—" Wasn't that why she had come back today. "You were an excellent worker. If you need a recommendation—"

"Thanks—" J. D. said cryptically. Grinning sheepishly, she threw back her shoulders, going to the door. "See you around."

"Goodbye—good luck, J. D." Pain snaked through her like a flame. To the closed door, she said quietly: "Thanks for it all."

The office seemed stuffy. She got up and pushed the window higher. Spring campus noises of cars and shouts stretched up to her. The tree limbs were covered with leaves and the green grass cushioned the sapphire blue of the sky. Students strolled together, laughing, talking, happy. Winter had changed into spring, a spring that had for her turned into an empty autumn.

Just before graduation on the way to the parking lot to go home, she saw J. D. from a distance, walking down the path with a dark-haired girl close to her side. The girl was looking up at J. D., smiling warmly, and J. D. was talking animatedly. J. D. looked happy. She was with her peer. And, she had found another challenge.

Penelope felt a sunken abyss within her gorged with sadness. Watching them, she wished it could have been different, knowing it could not. How could it have been? Not once had they spoken the word love. Suddenly she began to walk faster to the car, keeping her head turned away from the direction of *them*. She had to get home. Frizzle was waiting.

PLAY IT, BUT DON'T SAY IT

With Alice seated next to her on the front seat, Mattie Beatrice Brown slowly drove her sleek, black polished Lincoln Continental through the grubby niche of rough-tongued street licking out from the fang-toothed mouth of the ghetto. This section was a stunted pygmy of the city, but all hers to handle and manipulate. Possessiveness and pride claimed her as she gazed out the tinted windows at the people walking the streets—constituents to her—those black brothers and sisters.

The dwindling steel gray of a November twilight made the pedestrians blend like phantoms into the asphalt from which they seemed to emerge. To Mattie, they were her voting populace—poor, but significant nonetheless. She was grateful to all of them—the tall, thin, young, old men and women who had made *her*.

When she stopped for a red light, the policeman at the corner saluted in recognition. Directly behind him was a huge billboard with her picture looming big and brassy back at her. Her arm was raised high in a clenched fist and the lettering on the sign read: *Vote for Mattie B. Brown—U.S. Congresswoman, Third District—Voice of the Black People.* Two flags surrounded her, one the red, green and black liberation banner, and the other of red, white and blue.

"I like that billboard," Alice remarked, startling Mattie whose thoughts were turned upon herself.

"Hon?" She had forgotten Alice was beside her. One good thing about Alice, she knew how to keep quiet when Mattie wasn't in the mood to talk.

"The billboard—" Alice repeated, "I like it best of all."

The picture of Mattie on the panel stared back at her like a twin etched on paper. The drawing depicted her short, black hair in tightly curled ringlets peaking above a broad, brown face. Her almost flat nose tended to widen at the nostrils, flaring over a tidal wave of a mouth. With her piercing sharp dark eyes, she presented a formidable impression.

Back home in Dolsa, Georgia, they said that she was the spitting image of her father, big Thomas Jeffers Brown. He must have been the meanest black man on George Washington Carver Avenue where he ran a cluttered corner grocery store stocked with the poor blacks' staples of sodas, bread, crackers, bologna, rice and beans. Sundays, he was "called to preach" and served as the lay minister for the First Avenue Baptist Church. When Mattie got older, she began to think that his Sunday avocation was an atonement for cheating his own people during the week with marked-up prices and playing backroom politics with the local white rednecks for his own selfish gains.

Mattie hated her father's guts, but later, was glad she had inherited them. They were what she needed to survive in the manner she wanted, causing her to emerge victoriously from nothing to something. She had gone to Prairie View A & M and on to Howard University's Law School with the assistance of her family, work and scholarships.

When she received her law degree, she returned to Georgia but not to the small town of Dolsa, settling instead in a medium sized city. In Sanchersville, she opened a storefront law office perforating the heart of the ghetto. Here she made friends, learned to know and talk the tough, subtle everchanging secret language of the inhabitants, and became as hardened and slick as they. She worked to promote a high profile by keeping the pimps, bootleggers, whores and gamblers out of jail or getting them off with a light sentence. She gave cheap advice and charge minimum fees, hardly ever collecting on past due accounts. All of her machinations finally paid off. She was now U. S. Congresswoman Mattie Beatrice Brown who was on her way to Washington, D. C. She felt like shouting.

"Those people over there are waving to you—" Alice said, pointing.

Mattie's eyes followed the direction of Alice's finger. Upon seeing them, she flashed her big-toothed politician's smile and sounded her horn in appreciation. Jesus, it was *good* to *be* somebody!

"We really worked hard to win, didn't we?" Alice's small, thin voice came to her again from far away.

"Alice—" Mattie breathed in mock patience, "to win *anything,* you have to work hard." They *had* worked like poor folks' mules. She, in particular, morning, noon and night, holding meetings, giving speeches, shaking hands, garnering money in exchange for favors, making both ethical and unethical deals. A politician had to be a salesperson, wheeler-dealer and slickster. She had loved all of the grueling campaign, keyed up like a man with a perpetual hardon. The excitement was there of shrewd maneuvering. Luckily, she had an innate ability to quickly judge people—if they were honest, loyal, tricksters or leeches. This was difficult to do with black people who were born actors to make it in a white world.

"Well—I'm glad it's over. I'm tired—" Alice sighed wearily.

Mattie frowned, glancing at her. Alice did look a little pale and had lost weight, but she shouldn't be all *that* tired. Alice was just thirty-four, six years younger than she, and holding her age well. On the other hand, she surmised, Alice was by nature frail and dainty like her mother back in Dolsa. Maybe that was what had attracted her to Alice when she moved here seven years ago. Alice had an uncanny resemblance to Josie, a gentle, kind tiny woman who taught all grades in a one-room school, only to come home in the evenings to be voiceless in the background of Thomas Jeffers Brown. Alice was lighter in complexion than her mother, but had a similar round pretty face with delicate features. Alice reminded her of those supposed-to-be black dolls that she used to get for Christmas as a child—the ones with keen features, straight hair and painted brown.

Now on smoother streets leading away from the inner ghetto, Mattie drove faster, basking in the luxurious power of the car. Soon she pulled into the driveway of her house, a modest brick ranch type fringing the edges of her voting district. At this point, the black middle-class domiciles began, sprawling outwards away from the stink of the ghetto's mouth with greener pastures harboring fashionable homes.

"Here we are—" Mattie pressed the automatic device on her dashboard and the garage door eased upwards for the Lincoln to slide smoothly in.

When they entered the kitchen from the garage, the loud shrill of the telephone met them, pealing through the house. "Answer the private line for me, Alice," Mattie said, throwing off her coat. The house had already been lighted by the timer she had set. She had a phobia about entering dark houses. Being distrustful had become an intimate part of her nature.

Inside, the thought of food immediately nagged her. She was hungry. Unfortunately, eating was her weakness. Whether this was congenital, stemmed from growing up around a grocery store, or nerve induced, she sometimes wondered. The reasons seldom fretted her too much, for eating gave a soothing pleasure to her like a cat whose back was being stroked. She had gained ten pounds in three weeks before the election, sending out for hamburgers, french fries, Kentucky Fried Chicken, and thick milk shakes. To add to this conglomerate were the campaign fund raising dinners, extravagant lunches with key people in restaurants noted for their cuisine, and soul food suppers in greasy smelling joints where the street people frequented. A politician needed a good stomach.

"That was Con on the phone—" Alice disclosed, following her to the kitchen. "He wanted to remind you about your ten o'clock press conference in the morning at the Hyatt."

"Oh yeah—" Mattie grunted abstractedly, totally engrossed in peering at the various plastic containers and bowls in the refrigerator. She finally decided on the ham, potato salad and deviled eggs. Bringing out the food which she was aware that she should shun, a sting of resentment passed through her aimed at Alice. If Alice wouldn't keep her refrigerator stocked with already prepared food, she wouldn't be tempted. She liked to eat, but hated to cook.

"I'm going to get a drink. Want one?" Alice asked, going familiarly to the den off the kitchen.

Alice had helped design the house that Mattie had moved into after making enough money to leave the dark five-room apartment above her law office on Jungle Avenue. Reflecting upon this, Mattie began to speculate that Alice had deliberately positioned the bar near the kitchen for her own convenience.

"Mattie—do you want a drink?" Alice's voice octaved higher.

"Damnit, no!" Mattie yelled back, annoyed. Why in hell did Alice persist in asking? She knew that she didn't give a hoot about liquor, except sometimes for a light, dry wine with a particularly fine meal. Anyway, she had to keep her wits about her. Slicing the meat, the thought occurred to her that she ought to start locking up her booze, for Alice seemed to be hitting the sauce a lot lately.

Mattie piled her plate with food, got a sixteen ounce bottle of Coca Cola and sat down at the kitchen table. "Hey, Alice! You in there trying to drink up all my liquor?"

Alice came in with her usual Chivas Regal and water. She had put on some records and Roberta Flack's *Killing Me Softly* drifted languidly through the speakers like a creeping mist.

"Hum-m-m, I like that—" Alice murmured, leaning over Mattie, one arm around her shoulders, chin resting featherlight on top of her head— "and *you*."

"Umph!" Mattie grunted, reaching for more potato salad. It was heavily flavored with onions, the way she liked it.

Alice sipped the drink and began humming with the plaintive sound of the singer who was weaving a euphoric melody of love. "Dance with me—"

"Can't you see I'm eating?" Mattie snapped through a mouthful of food. Christ, stupid! Who wanted to get sentimental while eating?

Alice's lips brushed warm sunrays at the base of Mattie's neck, while her breath stirred a gentle rose-flung breeze. A spontaneous shiver of delight knifed through Mattie. Her free arm reached out and curved around the smallness of Alice's waist, bringing her to her side. "Babes— why don't you go and get comfortable for me?" Mattie's voice was huskily low.

Alice kept a gown, robe, toothbrush and other accessories in the private guest room for such times. She had the key to the house and knew more about the management and needs than the three-times-a-week housekeeper.

Suddenly Alice giggled over her glass.

"What's so funny, Babes?" Mattie asked, still using the confidential pet name for her woman.

Alice pulled out a chair and sat down. "I was just thinking: you were eating the first time I met you. Remember? At the NAACP benefit dinner at Mason Hall. Everybody had finished eating and gone into the auditorium waiting for you."

"Hell—the food was too good to leave. Anyway, it was a free speech," she snorted, wiping her mouth on a paper napkin.

Alice took another long drink from the tall frosted glass with a curved B on it. "I reminded you that people were waiting—"

A half smile crossed Mattie's lips. "That was my first formal introduction to the black *co-mune-ni-tee-e*, as my fired up young black activists call it," she laughed. "I gave *some* speech, didn't I? It was on a Black Woman's Search for Justice. Shame I hadn't thought about taping it at the time." Since then, she taped all her speeches, playing the tape over and over for herself and trapped guests. "Later, I got a spread in *Ebony*— Black Female Lawyer in the Ghetto."

Alice pulled out a pack of cigarettes from her jacket. "I was the one who got you that speaking engagement." She would never divulge to Mattie that she had been second choice when Judge T. Templeton could not do it.

Mattie sneered. "Oh, you and your little old committees." Alice was forever serving on community and social committees that investigated, planned, organized and gave functions. During that time, she was on the NAACP's program committee. Mattie supposed being a social worker required belonging to those frivolous committees that she personally termed as inconsequential in comparison to political committees which got right down to the nitty gritty—power and control.

Alice inhaled and heaved out a dragon's breath of smoke. The nicotine odor floated over Mattie's food and into her nostrils. "Goddamnit, Alice, you know I can't stand people smoking around me when I'm eating!"

"Sorry—" Alice hurriedly put out the cigarette and got up to empty the ash tray.

The loud rollicking sounds of a female rock group assailed the room:

"You got to lo—ve—ve—lo—ve—ve—yeah—yeah—yeah!"

"Yeah—yeah—yeah!" Alice chimed in, snapping her fingers and moving her hips in time with the rocking beat. "Let's dance—" she invited Mattie, twisting towards her in gyrating movements. .

Mattie gulped down the remainder of the Coca Cola and belched. Alice tugged at her hand. "Com'on—"

The thumping, pulsating music shook the kitchen walls. Laughing, Mattie stood up, moving her heavy body with the rhythm. She was amazingly light on her feet, and matched Alice's steps in unison, swinging her hips and bumping her. They got down, shaking, rocking, laughing unrestrainedly.

When the music ended, Alice breathlessly kissed Mattie who backed away in playful admonishment. "Watch out there. You're now kissing a U. S. Congresswoman!"

"Hum-m-m, and it's sure good!"

"Let's go to bed, Babes, so I can show you how *good* it *can* be!"

II

Mattie had a king-sized bed with a padded blue velvet headboard. When she made the selection, Alice had facetiously labeled it Mattie's bedtime monument. Now as she snuggled closely to Mattie's full, warm body, she was thankful for the huge bed which provided plenty of room for loving.

Clad in black silk pajamas, Mattie lay on her side, off-handedly stroking Alice's breast, as she talked in what amounted to a monologue: "I'm going to set that capitol on fire when I get there. Those white male congressmen are goin' to know who *this* black woman is inside six months. And the black me—en-n ain't never gonna see-e-e a more black bitch of a woman than this ole Sapphire!"

Alice tried to concentrate on Mattie's words above the wonderful feeling her hand was conferring on her breast. When Mattie got excited, her deep voice became lower, almost like a man's, and when Mattie finally relaxed, she would purposefully lapse into her black English— what she termed her first language. From past night interludes through the years, Alice knew Mattie was wound up and going to talk until she was tired. Shifting slightly, she reached over on the nightstand for her glass, reflected in the small glow of the nightlight like a frosted mirror. Slowly she sipped the liquor, savoring the taste of her relaxer.

"Yes—sir—ree! Those black me—en-n in Congress are going to see one *evil* black woman. Me! They're goin' to meet their match. Just like that Ike Smith who I beat. He ain't ne-ver goin' to forgit that a woman burned his ass in that election!" she guffawed, kicking up her heels beneath the covers. "I sure beat the hell out of that little fag."

Alice continued to drink, wishing Mattie would forget for a while her victories, hates, future and self, and remember her. "How do you know Ike Smith is a fag?" she pronounced the word distastefully.

"Hell—*everybody* knows it, including his wife!" Mattie retorted irritated by a question that she deemed a waste of time even to answer. "Goin' 'round all prim and prissy like he's got a stick stuck up in his behind all the time. So neat and clean you're 'fraid to even *breathe* on him. Polite as an undertaker."

"You shouldn't call him that, Mattie—" Alice chastised softly.

"I'll call him what I damn please—" The nerve of *her*. Alice and her not-wanting-to-hurt shit. Another facsimile characteristic of her mother. Nice to people, hiding behind genteelism, masking truth. A middle-class southern black woman's white female social acculturation.

"Suppose—" Alice bit her lip, clutching tightly to the glass balanced on her stomach—"somebody called you—"

"*Called me what?*" Mattie stopped her angrily, sitting upright in the bed like a mountain rumbling with the pent up fires of an impending volcano. "I dare you to *say* it!" she challenged, forgetting the ambiguity of it all embedded in her previous ruminations on genteelness versus speaking your piece.

Alice froze, closing her eyes against Mattie's wrath. Mattie's daring her to call it began six months after the NAACP dinner, one year after Mattie came to Sanchersville. There had been a snowstorm that evening, and in the south, if it snows, everything stops, for snow paralyzes a southern city. She was over to Mattie's and spent the night. The two of them sharing the one bed in the Jungle Street apartment. Mattie's hands had fumbled out for her in the square bedroom with the faded green paint. Within the circle of Mattie's arms, she had confessed in her ear: "I guessed it all along. That's why I wanted to meet you, to find somebody in this God awful secret black lesbian world with whom I could at least be myself—"

At those words, Mattie had pushed her away, hissing: "What are you *talking* about?"

"About you—me—*us*," Alice replied, a trifle frightened, for that was the first time she had seen the full vent of Mattie's temper.

"There is nothing to say about us," Mattie said coldly, the words as precise and incisive as a surgeon's knife. "As long as we are together—like this—I don't want to discuss it. In other words, don't *say* it."

Now as Mattie towered menacingly above her, a mixture of concern and anger invaded her, gnawing into the fibre of her being. This was representative of the times when she did not understand Mattie, or perhaps understood her too well, perceiving the weakness of her in this vulnerable spot which precipitated fear and defensiveness. Fear of what might become known and defensiveness against the possible hostility of those who discovered.

Suddenly Alice got up. "I'm going to get a drink—" A task which would involve a passage of time away from Mattie for her to calm down. And too, she wanted another refill. "Let me fix you one—" she suggested, thinking it might help—one way or another.

"You know I don't like the taste of liquor!"

"It's just that you seem to be all tight inside, restless—" Alice tried to explain, turning on the bedlamp to find her way to the den with her empty glass. At the bar, she drank a hasty straight shot, before mixing a double scotch and water. When she returned to the bedroom, Mattie was lying on her back, eyes glued to the ceiling, arms flung behind her neck.

"Phew-w-w, that stuff stinks!"

"No more than those damn onions on your breath—" the rebuttal came out of Alice's mouth like slippery greased lightning sooner than she had time to think. She placed her glass carefully on the table again and got back into bed. Why did Mattie have to make a profession out of abrasiveness—hardness? Was she afraid of tenderness—softness. Even with her lovemaking, it was strictly physical, insensitive in a way, detached, skillful mechanical movements to wind up a toy for carnal gratification. Had Mattie ever really loved anyone but herself? She doubted it, for love of self was too rooted in the seeds of her growth. She wanted to ask about the others in Mattie's life—those nebulous ghosts of whom she never spoke, but who Alice knew had been there. One has to get started somehow.

Coinciding with her thoughts, a warm feeling of compassion for Mattie flowed through her. "Let me soothe you—" she whispered in Mattie's ear, running her hands over the wide flabby spill of her overly abundant breast. "Help you to relax. Please."

Ignoring her, Mattie sprang up and began to pace back and forth in her lengthy, flatfooted movements on the deep pile of the rug. "The first thing I plan to do in Washington is to get on the committee for—"

With resigned disgust, Alice lay back, submerging herself in the only softness available at that time—the pillow. She was committed to wait for Mattie's urge. Mattie never thought of her—*her* needs. She was always the one who served, not the one to be serviced. She sought her glass and drank. The liquor helped to spin a vapor over what Mattie was saying.

"Shit—who knows? If I work at it hard enough, I might even become the first black and female vice president—"

Ambitious Mattie, Alice ruminated, the alcohol beginning to take a numbing effect, causing a languor which is sometimes miraculously accompanied by penetrating insight. Mattie might even make it as vice president. She had enough guts coupled with an ego that nurtures the will to succeed.

She, as different from Mattie, did not want to be anymore than what she was, nor do anymore than she was doing. What she wanted out of life was a lover who offered what a lover was supposed to: love itself. Some time ago, Mattie had told her that she was a dreamer—not pragmatic. Visions of dreamers were too frequently interred with their spirits.

As abruptly as she had gotten out of the bed, Mattie climbed back in. "Turn off the light—" she ordered gruffly.

Alice stole one long drink before rolling over in the boundless bed, fantasizing it as an endless beach of white cloud. Laughing, she snapped off the light.

"What's so funny—" Mattie grunted, arms pulling her close.

"Nothing—" Alice replied truthfully, for nothing was funny. She had simply laughed out of happiness, pleased that the time had come for Mattie to hold and love her. She made funny quick short lip marks on Mattie's face, impressioning herself on Mattie's forehead, eyes and mouth.

"Hum-m-m," Mattie murmured, smoothing her large hands up and down the length of Alice, "take off that gown—"

Alice struggled out of the flimsy pink nightgown and tossed it at the foot of the bed. Mattie wiggled out of the bottom of her pajamas and dropped them on the floor. Then she began to knead the brown nipples of Alice's breasts.

Alice closed her eyes, wishing Mattie would kiss her. Kisses were important. Soft kisses spoke of tenderness; medium ones of warmth; and the passionate of hunger and fire. Kisses too spoke of love.

"Hum-m-m, Babes—" Mattie moaned against Alice's right breast, lips closed around the nipple. Taking the top of the pear shaped cone into the wet cavern of her mouth, she sucked, licked and groaned with pleasure.

Alice's hands entangled into Mattie's hair, stroked and slid down her spine to the amazing flatness of her buttocks. She encircled each bottom cheek, squeezed and let one lone finger make a singular gliding bird movement from the base of her spine to the part in the twin-mound cleavage.

"Go-o-d, Babes, go-o-d—" Mattie's only term of endearment. She shuddered as Mattie's hand began to roughly work between her legs. Then Mattie sprawled on her back against the pillows and pulled Alice's small body on top of the huge mount of her own.

"OK—Babes—do your thing."

III

At ten a.m. the next morning, Mattie strode into the lobby of the Hyatt Hotel, impeccably dressed in Alice's wardrobe selection of a stylish beige woolen dress set off by a green jacket and scarf. She had handed Con her cashmere coat to hold, not trusting the coat hanger in the back of the room where the press was waiting.

Poised on the little platform stage in front, she quickly scanned the faces confronting her. The local reporters were recognized by flashing her intimate Tom Jeffers Brown smile. Most of them were white except for the one from *Jet* and another representing the NNPA. One white woman nearby caught her attention. She was husky, medium height, had short straight blonde hair which she kept pushing back from her face, and wore large owl framed glasses. Her tight-fitting jeans and denim jacket caused Mattie to frown disapprovingly, for the attire seemed an affront to her, not in deference to the occasion.

Confidently she turned to face the Third Estate. There was nothing, absolutely nothing, she liked better than being in the limelight before her public—the press and TV cameras. All over the country, people were seeing and listening to *her*—Mattie Beatrice Brown. During these high-lighted moments, she could imagine how a dictator felt, armed with the exuberant sensation of power engulfing him—an emotional vise more heady than the pangs of orgasm.

Con stood at the door, her coat draped over his arm, giving orders. He was performing those functions for which she paid him. She had heard that he sometimes called her "frustrating" and "temperamental" but what did she care, as long as he performed capably what he was assigned to do. At this stage, she still needed him. He was part of the black co—mune—ni—tee-e. Although middle-aged, he was youthful in appearance with his suave handsomeness. She wished he would shave off some of that beard encircling his mouth, making his lips look like a pussy. He looked extremely good this morning in his blue silk suit and splashy colorful hand-painted tie. By this, he made her look good too, communicating the fact that she could pick a staff.

The cameras came alive and the questions began, stock ones to which she smoothly gave answers, smiling as she did. She assumed the posture of coolness, confidence and self-assuredness. The queries were leveled at her:

"How does it feel to be a black woman elected to Congress?"

"Are you going to work with the Black Caucus?"

"What do you expect to accomplish?"

"Are you interested in any particular committees?"

She answered effortlessly, fluently, without hesitancy, aided by her innate gift for words. To the questions parried for which she wasn't ready to commit herself, she gave double-meanings that sounded like a plausible reply at the time, but later when the polish wore off, would shatter into puzzled pieces. Answers rolled off her tongue with well-oiled ease. She was a skillful politician, utilizing the most effective tool of her trade—words.

The woman in denim held up her hand. "Congresswoman Brown—"

"Yes—?" she smiled warmly, to show her woman-to-woman recognition. She, too, represented the minority of women.

"I'm Cathy Storm of the Gay Free Press—"

Mattie's smile froze into ice, body growing rigid from an inward caution warning. *How did she get in here?* she wondered to herself. She glanced reprimandingly at Con who was standing expressionless by the door.

"Ms. Storm—"

"Do you plan to support legislation in favor of homosexuals that would be especially beneficial to the triple jeopardy associated with black lesbians—"

Perspiration began to dampen Mattie's forehead and under her arms. She blamed the uncomfortable sweat on Alice. She shouldn't have worn the wool dress, but something lighter to cope with the lights and the room which she had instantly found to be too warm.

The reporter's eyes seemed to have grown as large and round as the brown frames of her glasses. With what Mattie interpreted to be a cynical smile, the woman repeated in a most deliberately explicit manner her question. The room seemed to become submerged in a stagnant pool of waiting.

Drawing herself up to her full five foot six inches, Mattie responded in a voice completely alien to her ears. "This is not my concern. You see, there are no such black women." After the statement, her lips pulled back over her teeth like a gorilla trying to smile.

The woman reporter's mouth flew open as the room was polarized in a split-second of shocked silence. When Mattie saw the woman's mouth

open again, she quickly turned to the man whose pencil was half raised
and said: "Next question—please."

IV

The evening's papers mocked her: *Black Congresswoman Claims No
Black Lesbians.* Within the sanctity of her home, Mattie had the answering
service monitor all her calls and cut off the ring of her private line.

Frantically she paced up and down the kitchen, slapping her forehead
and muttering repetitively to Alice: "God, out of all the *important* things
that I said, why in hell did they have to pounce on *that?*"

Alice had cooked dinner, beginning early in the day to prepare Mattie's
favorite prime beef roast. After she had looked at the press conference
on TV, she feared the worst. She thought the dinner would serve as a
partial balm to help soothe what she anticipated would be Mattie's strung
out nerves.

"Well—I think you could have given a better answer—" Alice said,
opening the oven door to check on the roast surrounded with potatoes,
onions and carrots. Her at-the-ready glass of scotch was on the counter.
She was a little tight, having started drinking after the TV conference
which had been in her opinion a disaster. In her haste to deny, Mattie
had made an ass of herself.

"What do *you* mean—*stupid?* I *don't* know any black *les-bi-ans!*"
The word came out in a clenched shriek, flung by force. "Do *you*—?"

She said it! Alice thought. *She has finally gotten the word out of
her mouth.* Alice looked at her contemptuously. Was she real? Or living
in a fantasy of wishful make-believe. What were *they? Play it—don't say
it.*

"Sure, I know some black lesbians and so do you. Only the nice middle-
class black women who *are* won't *admit* it. Careers, hiding behind husbands
and social status are more important in black life than admitting a same
sex preference." Alice picked up her glass and shrugged. "Besides, in the
long run, what good would it do? Coming out of the closet is more significant to white lesbians. That's why that woman asked you the question.
We black women in our struggle against racism planted the seeds for the
white women's movement. Now, I guess, it's time for *them* to do *us* a
favor. Liberate the so-called sex crazy black woman from her own hang-
ups. Making it so that if she's a lesbian, she won't be afraid to say or
feel deep within her that it is as good as shouting black is beautiful."

Mattie stared at Alice as if amazed that Alice could say so much, or
even carry a thought. Finally, drawing herself up, she said icily: "I have
no concern for black *or* white lesbians."

Alice finished her drink and moved to take the roast out of the oven.

"Dinner's ready—"

Seated at the table, Mattie generously began helping herself to the food. "Alice—you realize this shit is ruining my political career before I even get to Washington—" she continued, unable to forget what had transpired. "Lesbians—umph!"

"Mattie!" Alice shrilled, slamming her fist down hard on the table. "For God's sake, *what do you think we are?*"

A winter's blizzard crossed Mattie's face to film a sheath of ice. "You fool—" she uttered in disgust, "how do you figure *I* am one of *those?*"

"How do I—?" Alice echoed incredulously. Then in exasperation: "*Face* it—Mattie. You play it; you might as well *say* it."

Without warning, Mattie's hand shot out and struck her. Alice's face snapped around in a half arc from the blow. Surprise traumatized her, offsetting the sting of the slap. She gaped at Mattie who had calmly returned to eating. "You are unbelievable!" she blurted out incredulously, shaking her head in dismay. "Everybody knows, Mattie. They *know.*"

"Know *what?*" Mattie snapped, eyes narrowing. She fought to control her anger and the urge to drag Alice from the chair and shake her until her teeth fell out.

"What you *are.* Why do you think the woman was there—to ask?"

A sneer crawled over Mattie's face. "Alice—" she commenced with restrained patience, "they might *think* it, but they don't *know.* And if anybody accuses me publicly, I'll sue like hell!"

"You are denying yourself—"

"And *you*— Not to others?" Mattie struck back triumphantly.

"Actually—" Alice gave a small laugh, "no one has ever *asked.*"

"And if they did—?"

Alice looked down at her plate, a pinched frown between her eyes. "I don't know—. I just don't know—"

"Finish your dinner," Mattie commanded. "It's getting cold!"

"I'm not hungry anymore—I think I'm going home," Alice said, rising from the table.

"Be sure and lock the door behind you—" Mattie flung out to the departing figure. Turning back to her meal, she brought the food closer to her, spooning up second helpings of each dish. As she relished the succulent meal, her thoughts began seeking a plan of action, for Alice had given her a lot to think about.

V

Mattie phoned Alice early the next morning, inviting her to dinner after she finished work. All night she had explored step by step what she considered a major problem: her relationship with Alice. The problem had to be eradicated, for it threatened her survival as a politician and person.

By early morning, she had arrived at what she considered a workable and safe solution. The disposition settled upon negated her previous plans for Alice to go with her to Washington as a private secretary—of sorts. But if it were true what Alice had said about the knowing, then she had to leave her behind. She could not afford suspicion in an area extremely touchy to blacks. Lesbians were almost lepers. She had to be looked upon with unblemished pride by the black co-mune-ni-tee-e.

Taking Alice with her, whom people considered as her best friend, would lead to too much speculation. She knew a couple of friends elsewhere who lived together under the pretense of sharing an apartment or duplex. Thank goodness she had not succumbed to the idea of having Alice *live* with her.

In a strange way, she felt sad. She liked Alice in an unexciting way, and was going to miss her for a while. Alice had been her friend, companion, listening wall and lover. But after all, people destroyed faithful dogs when they had outlived their lives, didn't they? The cure for that was said to be go get another. What had to be done, had to be done. First things first, and Mattie Beatrice Brown would always be first with her.

When Alice arrived that evening, Mattie could tell that she had stopped by her after-work haunt, Big Lil's Lounge. The place was a favorite Happy Hour waterhole for the black bourgeois at five o'clock. Big Lil was a tub of a woman with a friendly yellow face who ran her place like a reigning black Pearl Mesta. She was the drinker's friend, confidant and mother, extending an open ear to problems made more sodden with liquor. Sometimes Mattie wondered about Big Lil—whether she was or wasn't. It was rumored she was.

The lingering odor of scotch and cigarette smoke from Big Lil's clung strongly to Alice, striking Mattie's nose in full force. It was all she could do to keep from blaring out: "You smell like a barroom fly." Resisting the indicting delivery, she graciously conjured up a smile and said: "I'm so-o-o glad you could make it."

Alice returned a little half smile familiar to Mattie, conveying that she was feeling good and guilty about it too. Mattie ignored it, determined that this was going to be a *good* evening. "Let me take your coat, Babes."

At this overture, Alice looked perplexed. She was accustomed to hanging up her own coat. Wasn't this home to her too? She watched Mattie walk over to the closet, her ample form hidden beneath the folds of African lounging attire. Alice had been around Mattie long enough to realize something was in the air. Beware of Mattie when she veered from her true self.

"Fix yourself a drink. I prepared a simply marvelous dinner."

"A drink would be fine—" Alice said, thinking she needed it to help cope with whatever was to come. When Mattie went out of her way to be charming, it was either to ask for something or deliver a swift kick while smiling. She preferred Mattie being her old, mean, self-centered self. That was the most honest part of her.

In the kitchen, Mattie proudly pointed to the food. "Look what I cooked for us—"

Alice held a double strength Chivas Regal for a sustainer. "Looks good—"

"Steak, baked potatoes, broccoli and a tossed salad—"

"Hum-m-m, nice—" Alice said, unimpressed. The menu was Mattie's only forte in the culinary department, except for bacon and eggs. She was impatient with anything else.

"I even set the table in the dining room—"

"So I see—" Alice remarked, looking into the room. "Best silver, dishes, candles—"

"For *us*, Babes—"

Alice swallowed her drink. Funny, even with all the drinks at Big Lil's, she couldn't get a buzz on yet. Too many warning signs.

"How's Big Lil?" Mattie asked randomly, placing thick steaks under the broiler.

Jesus-us, how did she guess I had been there? Simple, she knows your habit as you are standing here knowing hers, Alice Ryan, she apprised herself. "Big Lil's fine."

"I *must* stop by there sometime and thank her for helping me with the campaign." Then slyly: "She's quite a gal, isn't she?"

To this, Alice simply nodded affirmation. Seeing Mattie's quandary about leaving the steaks to finish the salad, Alice said: "Let me help you—"

"Oh, no-o-o! *I'm* doing this. You go on in and sit down."

Alice turned with relief from the mess of the kitchen with the coffee boiling over and broccoli half burning to take her seat at the long mahogany table covered with Mattie's best white linen tablecloth. Slowly she sipped her drink, eyes on the flickering candle flames conducive to intimacy, finding a mesmerizing warmth in them.

"Big Lil is a strange person—" Mattie said, bringing in the food.

Why was she harping on Big Lil? "Is she?"

"You stop by there quite a lot. Do you like her?"

"How do you mean?" Alice questioned testily.

"Personally—"

"*Everybody* likes Big Lil. She's warm, friendly and honest." *More than some can say about you,* her inner silent voice retorted.

Mattie made needless pilgrimages back and forth to the kitchen, showing her ineptitude at the task. "It's wonderful Big Lil can run that place all alone without a man's help."

"She has a good business sense—" Alice spread her napkin over her lap. "And I don't know if she's a lesbian," she added perceptively.

Mattie flung her a grim look. "Alice, I didn't ask for that."

"You didn't have to. I just guessed—" Alice said too sweetly. "Shall we eat?"

"A very nice dinner," Alice complimented her, watching Mattie put more logs in the living room fireplace. The fire was lit only for Mattie's few special occasions, like the expensive after-dinner brandy she had brought out. It would all have been very nice if she didn't know Mattie like she did.

Leaning back in her favorite chair, Mattie sighed. "Ah-h-h, if this could last forever, Alice. Evenings like this with you."

Alice said nothing. The fire cracked as the flames leaped into a dance of warmth. Mattie moved out of her chair to come over and sit beside her on the couch.

"Babes—it's going to be a long, hard road for me ahead in Washington."

"I know—"

"I'm going to have *double* problems now. There and *here.* So, I've been thinking. What I need is someone I can *trust* to take care of *this* end for me—where my voters are."

Alice clutched the brandy glass, then set it down on the coffee table. The taste of it had suddenly turned sour. She needed a cigarette. The inhaling and exhaling would help her breathing, keep her calm.

"I've decided, as much as I hate it, not to take you to Washington with me. I need you *here—*"

The flick of the gold lighter kept on the coffee table was sharp as an electric shock in a room of steel. Alice deliberately took her time, dragging hard on the cigarette before she blew out a reeking stream of smoke directly into Mattie's face.

Mattie did not flinch, nor did the manufactured look of pleading for understanding vanish from her face. "I can *trust* you, Babes, more than anybody. You can keep an eye on Con for me. I believe my soul that he deliberately let that—that woman in the press conference to embarrass me. And, I need you, Babes, to see that the housekeeper does her job and to keep an eye on the office. I'll put you on the payroll—" Mattie felt pleased. Paying Alice would make it appear more real, and alleviate any twinge of compunction she might develop. This way was the best. Eventually she would get rid of her completely. There would be no one around to cause speculation. If she had to give up sex, she would submerge herself in work.

"In other words," Alice began slowly, frowning, "you're trying to get rid of me. I may become an embarrassment—"

"Of course not, Babes!" Mattie exclaimed, throwing up her hands in feigned bewilderment. "How could you even *think* a thing like that? All we've been together in the past—"

"Because I know *you*, Mattie. How important your work is to you. Your drive—ambition—"

Mattie looked in confusion at Alice, watching her cooly smoking a cigarette. This was an Alice she could not fathom. She had considered Alice to be a trifle light upstairs, but she was presently demonstrating that she had more sense than she had been given credit for having. Alice, like her mother, underneath it all knew Thomas Jeffers Brown, understood her.

"There—you see! Since you *do* know how much my work means to me, this proves that I can't do without people I can trust—" Mattie seized upon her words, turning them to her own advantage.

Alice gave her a long disdainful look before putting out her cigarette and getting up. "Don't worry, Mattie. I won't ruin you, and I know how to keep my mouth shut."

"Babes—" Mattie looked at her in abashment, feeling a hollowness in her stomach. She would have rather there been a fight, anger—or even tears and pleadings. These she could deal with, not this deadly coldness exhibited by Alice. It wasn't even a contest.

"I wish you luck—" Alice said, getting her coat.

Mattie went swiftly across the room to her. "You *are* going to take care of this end for me, aren't you?" The question turned itself into an entreaty.

"I don't know. I'll have to think about it." She would not have to ponder long. If there was to be a break, it was best to have it over—clean, no hanging-ons. Mattie would finish it anyway when her usefulness was over. It would have been nice to stay with her, glory in her triumphs, be there to cushion her defeats. Only it takes more than one to make an equation of love.

"Think it over, Babes—" Mattie's arms went about her.

Alice stood rigid in the embrace. The kiss on her mouth was like the surface of a stone. She opened the door, smiling sadly. "Just remember, Mattie, play it—don't say it. And you'll be safe."

Mattie stood for an indeterminable time frowning at the closed door.

Then the pangs of hunger as powerful as the cramps unexpectedly seized her. Automatically she went to the kitchen. Without preliminary thought she began to pull out dishes of food and place them on the table. Then she sat down and started to eat. She ate on and on into the night, until the deep hollow well within her had seemingly been filled—for a while. It was only then the lingering thoughts of Alice went away.

THE PLAY

Robin was quiet at the table with Lynn, trying to finish the soul food dinner of beef tips, rice and black-eyed peas they had ordered. She knew this was going to be another one of those outré Saturday nights similar to the others, when Lynn got the urge to eat out, mingle with people, do something. It was also one of those set agonizing nights Robin hated.

The restaurant had only a few diners, but the cocktail lounge off to the side was beginning to fill with people. From this part could be heard a combo threading out musical sounds. The dimly lit lounge seemed suffused in an intricate web of talk and laughter. It was in this direction Lynn kept turning to look.

"You aren't eating anything, hon," Robin rebuked her gently, comparing her plate, at least half finished, to Lynn's barely touched one.

As if to satisfy her, Lynn began a pretense of forking up her food. Robin's gaze centered on Lynn's hand with the red painted nails making five blood-stained eyes on the end of a nectarine colored hand. She did not want to look up to the face fashioned in the delicate beauty that made her a black model. She loved Lynn—too much—knowing that this caused her to take more than she should.

Suddenly Lynn said: "Excuse me. I'll be right back." Standing up, her clear brown eyes looked down at Robin, softening for a moment, almost transmitting a plea.

Robin recognized the appeal for understanding; this was Lynn's way of saying despite what happens, it's you. *Act one has commenced; curtain going up,* Robin announced to herself. Her head began to ache in a dull throb. To Lynn, she said: "All right," for Lynn was going anyway.

The waitress came over to the table. "Anything else?"

"I'll have more coffee, and the check, please," Robin said.

The waitress tore off the bill from her little yellow pad, placed it face down on the table and went for the coffee. Robin looked at the slip and stuck a bill beneath it. Reappearing, the waitress refilled her cup, took the money and told her to come back.

After what was a short time to Robin, Lynn returned with a man. He was six feet tall, lean with a smooth brown handsome face set off by a thick moustache and small goatee. The trousers of his pink summer suit were tightly fitting, exposing the full imprint of his privates. His white sports shirt was opened at the collar where the top of black matted chest hair entangled like an underbrush.

Lynn's eyes were overly bright, vacant, pin-pointed in a nebulous space beyond. "Robin—this is Lucius. He wants to buy us a drink."

Lucius smiled with strong, white teeth. "Hi, Robin, how you doin'?" he greeted, sprawling like a lion in the chair between them. He spread his thighs wide, exhibiting more the manhood bunched between them. When he saw Robin's furtive glance to and away from the front of his pants, he grinned slyly. Taking a silver case out of his pocket, he offered them a cigarette.

Robin refused, while Lynn took one and waited for him to light it. "Are you going to eat anymore?" Robin asked Lynn.

"No, I've had enough—"

Robin looked across the room and signaled the waitress to clear the table. The food was cold and Lynn really wasn't interested in eating.

"Why don't y'all come over to the lounge and have a drink?" Lucius invited. His voice was deep, richly melodious, like a black Delta preacher.

"Ok with you, Robin?" Lynn nervously puffed on the cigarette, exhaling but not really inhaling.

A question of indifferent protocol, Robin reflected, watching Lynn use the cigarette for a stage prop, knowing she did not smoke except on these occasions. Resigned, she ran the palms of her hands over the sixty-dollar Bewitte slacks that Lynn had bought for her at a discount when modeling for the store. Artists such as she, who sold paintings once or twice a month, couldn't afford expensive clothes.

"All right—"

Locked in a blind vise, she followed them to the darkened cavern of the lounge. Here, music was being made by three spaced-out musicians working on a piano, drum and saxophone. Lucius led them to a table near the bandstand.

"What do you want?" he asked, flashing his Billy Dee Williams smile again, cigarette a smoking white coil between brown fingers.

"I'll have an old-fashioned—" Lynn replied, smiling her prettiest back at him.

Robin remembered the script always called for old-fashioneds. Lynn told her that old-fashioneds made her feel sexy. "I'll have a scotch and water—"

"Right-on, lovely ladies. Be right back—"

When he left, Robin said stingingly to Lynn: "It doesn't take you long."

Lynn's carefully circled eyebrows, ringed beneath with blue eyeshadow, lifted in a slight frown. "Long?"

"You know what I mean. To find one." Why should it, she reasoned, as pretty as Lynn was.

"He just wanted to buy me a drink—" Lynn put out her cigarette, then fidgeted with the ash tray. "He's good looking, isn't he? Real masculine—"

The word reverberated in Robin's mind like an accusation. *Masculine.* What *she* wasn't. What Lynn was driven to seek from time to time like a therapy: to prove herself, stabilize her self-concept. She was only bisexual, which was better, more normal, halfway sane.

"I brought a friend back—" Lucius stood over them with drinks and his friend. "This is Chester—"

Chester was medium height, a dingy yellow, wore tinted glasses and had a dull face. He appeared to have just come from the barber shop where his stiff-bristled hair had been cut too short. The heady perfumed odor of shaving lotion made a sweetish vapor around him. "Hello—" he said, taking a swig from a glass of beer in his hand.

"These beautiful young ladies are Lynn and Robin. Sit down, man."

Chester edged beside Robin, placing his beer before him. He had on a flat, round gold wedding band. Lucius raised his glass: "Here's a toast to all of us who get the most! Hah, hah!"

Lynn's answering laugh resounded like a hollow broken egg. Chester's expression was void as he cast his eye at Robin.

She always picks that kind, Robin thought, *macho, aggressive, openly offensive.*

The band gave a screaming blare and a short, chubby man dressed in an all-white suit with hair frosted blonde pranced out on the stage. "Oh, God, there's Bernard. Or should I say Bernadine," groaned Lucius.

"He can sing," Chester praised lamely.

"*It* can sing—" Lucius guffawed, throwing an arm around the back of Lynn's chair.

Robin felt hot and cold, fixing her gaze stoically on Bernard. The combo struck up a blues number and Bernard opened his mouth in a wail about can't get enough of that stuff. The sexy lyrics and rhythmic rocking beat fired the audience to shout: "Sing it, Bernard! Git down-n-n—"

Spurred on by the with-it spectators, Bernard shook his fat hips, licked a red wet tongue and rolled his eyes lasciviously:

> Can't get enough
> Oh no no no-o-o
> Of that good stuff
> From my baby's muff!

"Bulldaggers, fags and flies, I *do* despise—" Lucius snorted, eyes on Bernard.

Robin bit her tongue and picked up her scotch, downing it quickly. The drink goaded her to speak: "How can you tell—who's what?"

"Baby, I can spot 'em *anytime*. All she-he's and he-she's. What the women need is some good man lovin', and the men ought to be castrated and thrown in the goddamed river!"

"I want another drink—" Lynn's voice was tight. Her eyes avoided Robin as she squeezed Lucius's arm.

"Sure, pretty momma, anythin' your li'l old heart desires," Lucius replied, getting up and brushing his hand across the fly of his trousers.

When Robin saw Lynn turn her chair around to watch the bandstand, she realized Lynn was letting her know that she was on her own. This gift of independence was by Lynn's logistics supposed to be therapeutic for her, teaching her how to relate to men.

Smoothing his tie, Chester turned to Robin. "Is this your first time here?"

"No. We usually splurge once in a while and eat out someplace." More than once in a while if Lynn's conscience got out of hand and needed assuaging.

"Are you related?"

"Roommates—friends—" for a long time. She wished that she could see his eyes shaded by the glasses. He had a funny square jaw. A comic strip character. Perhaps she looked weird to him: too tiny, short, mediocrity bathed in a desert tan. She would like to sketch him.

She must have been staring hard, for he said: "What are you thinking?"

"About sketching you."

"You're an artist?"

"Yes."

"I always wanted to do something artistic. Only, as my luck runs,

I ended up teaching manual arts in junior high school," he laughed deprecatingly.

"There's nothing wrong with that," she said gently. And because she had to, she continued: "What does your friend do?"

"Lucius? He's not a close friend—" he paused, taking a sip from his beer. "A little of everything, I guess. He's a real go-getter—"

Bernard finished singing and the audience yea-a-a-d and clapped. Lucius emerged through the crowd, leading the waitress with a tray loaded with a second round for all. The combo started a slow number and Lucius motioned to Lynn to dance. Robin watched him holding her close. Lynn's head rested on his shoulder. Her eyes were closed, lips half parted and hips clamped against his, moving intimately. Hurt racked through her like a volcano.

"Would you like to dance?" Chester asked politely.

Not trusting her voice, she moved her head negatively. When Lucius and Lynn rejoined them, both were breathing heavily. "Drink up, folks!" Lucius urged. "There's more where that came from."

While they drank, Lucius dominated the conversation, peppering his chatter with jokes and hidden innuendos. Finally he suggested: "Let's all go for a ride to the beach. I'd take you to my pad, but somebody's using it now. I don't believe in interruptions—" he winked.

"Sounds great to me—" Lynn agreed, fishing for the cherry in her glass.

"In whose car?" Robin inserted.

"Mine—. I got a Lincoln Continental outside big enough for all of us and then somemore." For verification, he turned to Chester: "Don't I, man?"

Chester nodded. "Sure have. A '76 too."

"I'm not leaving my Volkswagon," Robin said stubbornly.

"Oh, we can just pick that li'l old thing up and put it in my trunk," Lucius roared, slapping his knee. "Tell you what, you and Chester follow us to the beach. Then we can all get in my car and listen to some tapes and whatever."

"It's fine with me," Chester conceded.

"Well, what are we waiting on?" Lynn breathed excitedly. "I might even take a swim!"

"In the nude, baby?" Lucius haunched her, eyes slits of speculation. "Com'on, let's go, y'all."

II

The Volkswagon appeared a miniature parked behind Lucius's black Continental. Lucius had bought beer, scotch and a bottle of ready mixed old-fashioneds for Lynn. He had also picked up a couple of joints. "When I party, I par-te-ee!" he exclaimed, producing his purchases. "I want ever-r-rybody hap—pee!"

The smell of the joint Lynn and Lucius were smoking drifted back to Robin. She had hoped Lynn would refuse as she had. Chester simply nursed a beer. She tried to allay her thoughts by sipping scotch and concentrating on the Al Green tape. Only nothing was working. Her mind still focused on Lynn and Lucius, cuddled together on the front seat. Watching them, she had not become aware that Chester had put his arm about her, not until his lips brushed her cheek.

Why does she put me through this torture? Robin wondered. Was it worth it? To have to keep Lynn? She had nothing to prove to *herself.* She was not bisexual. She was what she was. Men did not enter the picture at all.

"Are all artists this quiet?" Chester breathed in her ear.

She shuddered at the scent of his beer breath. He could have been less proletarian with his drinks. She hated the smell of beer. "I guess I think too much." Wasn't that what Lynn had told her advising: *It's more fun doing sometimes than thinking about it.*

Doing was Lynn's activity now, not thinking about her on the back seat watching a perfectly obnoxious stranger of a man making love to her. It was as if she didn't exist. Or was this a form of Lynn's sadistic torture for her? Maybe Lynn was getting her kicks twofold: from him and the secret knowledge of her female lover watching helplessly on the back seat.

The feel of Chester cupping her breast startled her. His mouth clamped over hers like a wet hand, stifling, oppressive. She jerked her head away to stop the roaring waterfall in her ears.

"What's wrong?" he whispered.

"I don't feel well. I need some air—" She opened the door, throwing out her drink, and stumbled into the night, escaping Lynn's moans of pleasure. She began to walk rapidly, going nowhere, somewhere along the jagged beach line. The dark stretching boundless water was lit with moonlight flecks of dancing silver fairies.

She did not know that he had followed until he called: "Robin, are you all right?"

The gentle concern in his voice made her stop and wait for him. "Yes—"

"If you want to walk, we'll walk."

They moved together slowly, in silence, feet making cookie crunching sounds in the sand. Eventually he said: "I wasn't going to do anymore than you wanted me to—"

"I shouldn't have come out here—with *them,*" she murmured as if to

herself, thinking she had not played her part very well. She never did.
"Lucius is like that, always trying to prove himself with women. He's usually successful." There was a mixture of pride and envy in his words.

They stopped and sat down on the gritty, powdered sand. She leaned her head on her knees and closed her eyes, listening to the ocean waves making their distinctive splash of sound. The warm salt air permeated her nostrils like ammonia, purging her. She became heedful of the man beside her—a remote adjunct. He was trying to be kind.

As though conscious of her inward turmoil, he reached out, absently running his hand through her hair and down over her face. His ring left an invisible scratch on her cheek.

"You're married—" she stated matter-of-factly.

"Uh-huh."

He gave no more and she did not pry. After all, what did it matter. She stayed still, trapped in the abyss of her rushing dark thoughts. Suddenly she exhaled a sigh. "I'm leaving. Can I drop you someplace?"

"Home—"

They walked past the long sleek silent car in which now no forms could be seen. Abruptly anger blazed within her like a fire, inflating her mind into a tired, helpless latent scream. Torn with jealous fury, she stumbled into her car, pressing down hard on the accelerator, causing a loud emission of fumes and motor noises. And just before she backed out of the cove, she leaned her weight on the horn and blew and blew: *Ah-h-ho-o-o-o.* The blaring tore through the night like a painful cry of a suffering animal bellowing out a wounded rage.

III

At home in bed, she lay quietly, waiting for Lynn. There was a time when she cried. Now the tears had all ended and only a dry desert of pain remained. She knew it was going to be a long night until Lynn came home again to close down the curtain on their sporadic dream. A travesty laden with the pathos of self-mockery.

HOME TO MEET THE FOLKS

Roz was irritable as she sat across the table from Marge in the holiday-filled coffee shop off the turnpike. The sounds of loud voices and ringing jingle of the cash register resounded sharply against her ears, causing her to become more impatient to leave. Hurriedly draining her cup, she frowned at Marge, who had hardly touched the coffee that she just had to have before traveling any farther.

"Look, hon, we have to hurry. Mom's real together about serving Thanksgiving dinner on time."

"All right—" Marge replied, giving her a faint smile. "Maybe we should have started earlier."

"We *could* have, but *you* had to sleep longer. Remember?"

Picking up her cup, Marge looked away. "I was tired—"

"Yeah, I know," Roz said, grimly.

In silence, Marge concentrated on finishing her coffee. Then, putting her cup down with a finality, she asked pointedly: "Roz, do you think she'll like me?"

Roz's face softened as she gazed back at Marge's round childlike face with the wide-spaced green eyes over a nose of pepper freckles and long brown hair framing each side like a curtain. "You *bet* she will! Mom'll go crazy over you like I did the first time."

A tired middle-aged waitress came wearily over to them. "If you don't want anything else, that'll be fifty cents," she said, taking out her yellow order pad while looking at Marge.

"*I* have it," Roz snapped, quickly searching her pockets. "Here—" She

She threw a dollar bill on the table. "Keep the change." Anger again had bred extravagance within her. It was another repeated moment in their long relationship of affronts when in company with Marge. She was black, and naturally, black women had no money.

"Let's go—" she said, brusquely.

Marge got up to follow Roz out the door, ignoring the curious stares directed at them. Roz always drew attention in a crowd. She was tall and slim with a huge curly Afro like a crown above her smooth sharp-boned ebony face. There was an air of regalness about her in the proud way she carried herself, straight and lofty as an African queen.

"We should be at Mom's in an hour," Roz surmised, climbing into the driver's seat of the small blue Toyota.

Marge, occupied with her thoughts, got in quietly beside her. Roz reached over and patted her hand. "You'll like Mom. She's a shining Moynihan example of a hard-working fine black woman," she laughed. Then in a more serious tone: "Hon, I wanted you to come and meet the family."

Like married people, Marge reflected. Once she had a family whom she went home to visit on holidays. Once—until they found out. Now after a year of togetherness, Roz was her only family.

Roz headed the car back to the highway and Stubbenville where she was born and grew up and left for good. For a long while, the car's motor was the only sound between them. Much later as Roz peered out the windshield at the overcast sky, she murmured uneasily: "It looks like snow's on the way. I hope it holds off until we get there."

Marge looked at Roz, wondering why she was worried about snow. Roz could handle anything—leaky faucets, stuck windows, keyless locks. To her, Roz was uncanny in her ability to perform, handle outrageous situations, *do.* Roz was a marvel. A feeling of adoration invaded her. She reached over to trace a delicate little nameless pattern on the back of Roz's hand, fascinated as usual with the color contrast of black over white.

"Look out there, honey," Roz chuckled. "What are you trying to do? Make me have an accident or stop the car?"

"The last isn't a bad idea at all—" Now Marge's hand caressed the outline of Roz's leg in the corduroy pants.

"No time for seductions— ' Roz admonished. "We're going home to Thanksgiving dinner and meet the folks."

"Meet the folks—" Marge repeated, closing her eyes, trying to picture Roz's folks. "What about your brother, Louie? Think we'll get along?"

"Like *crazy!* Louie gets along with everybody," Roz grinned. "It'll be good seeing him again. He used to call himself looking after me. Keep-

ing me out of scraps and places where I had no business being. Imagine!
And Louie only two years older than I. He's coming all the way from
L.A."

Marge thought of Louie who had two years ahead of Roz's twenty-
eight and five after her twenty-five, and if he looked like Roz. Then she
wondered about Roz's mother—the woman who had taught six grades
in a one-room rural school outside Stubbenville and helped Roz's postal
clerk father buy a house and educate Roz and Louie at the black state
college. Roz's mother was retired now, seven years after her husband's
death. For a skittish moment, Marge's train of thought lingered briefly
on her parents—the father who was a retired army colonel, and the spirit-
less mother who was now his sole command.

"Sleepy?"

Roz's husky voice severed her ruminations. "No, just thinking."

"About me, I hope!"

Marge rubbed her face against the rough plaid of Roz's plaid mackinaw
jacket. "Always, about you—us."

"You don't have much longer to think now," Roz said, giving her a
fleeting side kiss. "We're almost there."

II

Marge stood in the background as Roz's mother greeted her with hugs
and kisses. "Baby—I'm so glad to see you!"

It's good to see you too, Mom," Roz said, kissing her back.

"Louie's already here. And guess what? With a wife!"

Roz's face showed surprise. "Louie's *married?*"

"Uh-huh. Didn't tell a *soul*. Not even his own mother!" Suddenly
she looked hard at Roz. "You aren't married *too*—are you? I'd like to
have at least *one* wedding in the family. Do it up right."

"No—" Roz smiled weakly. A lie. She was, in *her* way. She felt like
a traitor to Marge. "Mom, I brought a friend home with me—Marge Hall."

Now Roz's mother focused on Marge in the dimness of the hallway.
Marge looked back at her, seeing a little piece of Roz mirrored in the
piercing dark eyes set in an aristocratic face. She had on a beige wool
dress almost the color of her skin, and Marge recognized the yellow har-
vest apron tied around her with Thanksgiving on it. Roz had sent the
apron as a gift this time last year when they did not come. There was
the aura of the old schoolteacher dignity about her in the studied manner she carefully chose her words.

"How do you do, Miss Hall. I'm pleased to have you as a guest."

"Thank you, Mrs. Parrish. It's nice to meet you after hearing Roz
talk so much about you." Under the woman's sharp scrutiny, she was

glad that she had worn her best pantsuit instead of the jeans Roz had told her to throw on.

"Is that Sis?" The voice coming into the room was jubilant.

"Louie!"

Marge, still feeling like an outsider, watched Roz and Louie embrace each other. Louie was short and heavyset, and had a thick beard that covered half of his face. He made her think how nice it would have been if she had a brother or sister.

"Hey, Kitty—Sis's here!" Louie bellowed out a roar that must have penetrated to not only Kitty upstairs but the Lord too.

Immediately Kitty came down to join them. She was attractive in a sexy way with a long African print dress wrapped in layers around her ample curves and matching earrings knifing down the sides of her peach colored cheeks. As Marge acknowledged the introduction, she could feel Louie's admiring male gaze, while sensing the outward hostility in Kitty's frown.

I don't want your man, she wanted to say to the girl, just his sister. A sensuous emotion began to flood her like the heat from loving, warming her with a natural brilliance that made her want to reach out and press herself close, ever so close to Roz.

"Well, let's not stand here all evening," Roz's mother laughed happily. "Louie, take the girls' things upstairs and put them in Roz's old room. I'm going to finish dinner."

As soon as Louie deposited their bags and left, Roz fell over on the bed, kicking up her legs gleefully. "Just think! Here *you* are in the room I grew up in!"

Marge looked around the room which had housed and kept Roz's secrets, happiness and sadness. It looked as if it would always be kept for Roz. The cubicle bedroom was half swallowed by a full bed covered with a blue chenille bedspread that contrasted with the pink striped wallpaper. A chest of drawers held a square mirror and picture of a younger Roz in her college cap and gown. On the antique round marble table by the window was a vase of fresh yellow chrysanthemums giving the room life and warmth.

Filled with the beauty of the moment, Marge fell on the bed beside Roz, and instantly knew the familiar circle of Roz's arms around her, pulling her into and against her. She trembled as Roz's lips closed like a heated blanket over her thin mouth. A knowing tremor made her ache and just as she moved to position herself beneath Roz, a knock sounded on the door.

"Mom's got dinner ready—" Louie called.

"Shit!" Roz giggled. "Just as we were going to christen the bed!"

"Oh, well. We'll have *all* night long—" Marge whispered against Roz's throat.

"Hum-m-m, and it's going to *be* all night long!" Roz promised.

III

They sat down at the dining room table that had a history of Sunday and holiday family dinners. The table's white linen cloth was set with turkey, dressing, candied sweet potatoes, collard greens, macaroni and cheese, along with homemade rolls and jellies.

"This is certainly a *special* Thanksgiving for me to have *all* my children home," Mrs. Parrish said, smiling broadly. "God has really blessed me."

"He's blessed us all, Mom, to have a wonderful mother like you!" Louie said, getting out of his chair to make a big production out of carving the turkey.

Marge looked at Roz's mother at the head of the table filling their plates with more food than they needed. Automatically she reached to help pass the plates around. The food smelled good to her, reflecting the festive holiday preparation. Last Thanksgiving, they ate in a restaurant.

"And I am thankful to God for giving me another daughter—Louie's wife. Maybe soon, I'll have another son."

"Don't count on it, Mom," Roz winked. "I'm not the marrying kind."

"Oh, Roz, you just haven't met *the* one yet," Kitty chimed in.

"*I* can fix her up!" Louie offered, digging hungrily into his food. "I know a real nice guy who—"

"Not interested, Louie—" Roz cut in, laughing.

"Honey, let *me* tell *you*, there ain't *nothing* like having a *man*—" Kitty said, proudly squeezing Louie's arm.

Marge kept her eyes down on her plate, thinking why don't they leave her alone. Now the voice suddenly aimed at her belonged to Kitty.

"Marge, are you engaged—or something?"

Afraid to trust her voice, Marge simply shook her head. She knew there must be something else for them to talk about. Always in the company of straights, there was the inevitable conversation of engagements and marriages leveled at single women. Her father's voice entered her thoughts: *Get a boyfriend—it's healthy.*

"You two work at the same place?" Kitty went on, curiously.

"Yes—" Marge said, looking up, annoyed at the subtle probing. "I'm a women's sportswear buyer for the store and Roz is in personnel."

"We live together too—" Roz added, helping Marge.

Kitty's eyes widened. "You *live* and work together? My! You two must get along *real* well. That's more than some married people can do. How did *that* happen?"

"It just happened," Roz replied shortly. "Perhaps we understand each other better than some married people."

"Apparently—" Kitty murmured, sarcastically.

A queasiness permeated Marge's stomach. What was Kitty targeting for? Had she guessed? There was always the nagging fear that someone had guessed—or *knew*.

"My daughter's going to find herself a nice young man someday. You just wait. The good Lord makes all things happen in good time," Mrs. Parrish predicted.

IV

Refusing help with the dishes, Roz's mother made them go into the living room where they lounged, satiated with the big meal. Louie had produced a fifth of scotch which had put him into a festive mood.

"Hey, girls, let's go out on the town. I want the homefolks to meet my wife."

"You and Kitty go on," Roz said tiredly. "You *flew* here, remember? We drove."

"Aw, what's a little eight-hour drive?"

"Go on with them, Roz," Marge urged, getting up yawning. "It'd be nice for you to see your old friends again. I'm going to bed."

As Roz watched her bid them goodnight, her eyes sent Marge a hidden kiss. She wanted to tell her that she would be up soon. It wasn't a bed without the two of them together.

When Marge left, Louie abruptly turned to her. "Why in hell do you want to live with a *honky?*"

The question was like a blow, causing Roz to brace herself against the sofa. Reaching for more ice, she replied tight-lipped: "She's my friend."

"Frankly, *I* don't think *any* white person can be a friend," Kitty said cooly. "I teach with them during school hours, and after that, I go *my* way and they go *theirs*. It's less complicated that way."

"Why would she want to live with *you?*" Louie continued to question her. "White people don't need *us* for friends. What's she trying to prove? How liberal she is?"

Kitty emptied her glass and reached for the bottle. "Maybe she's funny. White women are really into *that* now, I hear. With this women's liberation crap going on—"

Roz felt the hot tightness within her curling into a whorl of anger. Voice strained, she asked: "Funny? How do you mean, *funny?*"

"A *lesbian*, sweetie," Kitty said, eyebrows raised mockingly. "A woman lover. I hear some of them *love* to get it on with black women," she giggled.

She knew that she should say something. But she couldn't think of anything to say. Defend, deny, admit. To stall for time, she slowly sipped the expensive scotch Louie had generously poured into her glass, letting it wet her mouth, soothe her fury, help the moment.

Marge felt that Kitty was baiting her. Why couldn't she just leave her alone? She felt helpless, frustrated because she couldn't take care of her own. She should defend Marge—the one she loved. In this way, she was dishonoring her. A battle can't be won with a fight.

"If she *does* make a pass at *my* sister, I'll beat the shit out of her—" Louie growled, furiously.

Rockets exploded in Roz's head as she heard the words. Shaking with uncontrollable fury, she stood up to confront him. "If you lay a hand on her, I'll kill you!"

In the galvanized silence that followed, she faced them adamantly. *Now they knew.* She felt strong with relief. Her eyes firmly met the shocked stares which slowly changed to loathsome understanding.

"I'll be damned," Louie cursed, softly. "*She* mean that much to you?"

I've cut the family ties, Roz said to herself. I'm out there now by myself in the jungle. Just me and Marge. "Yes—" Her gaze defied him. It was never going to be like it used to be between them. She could tell by the way he was looking at her with a mixture of disbelief, puzzlement, contempt.

"My sister—a—*queer!*" he spat out.

"Caused by *white* pollution," Kitty broke in. "It's a white trick for black genocide. Lesbians can't get babies. Black women should have black men to get black babies and build a strong black nation."

"I'm not interested in males—black or otherwise. Nor do I want to have any babies. I just want to live my own life, go my own way, do my own thing with whom I *choose.* Like you."

"Like *us!*" Kitty almost screamed. "How *can* you?"

"As a goddam *lesbian,*" Louie retorted incredulously. "Christ! I can't own no sister who's a bulldagger. You're not a woman—"

"Then, what *am* I, Louie?" Roz asked evenly. "I'm just as much a woman as your wife."

"What? How can you say that? You—" Kitty jumped up, springing across the room at Roz. "Don't you compare *me* to what *you* are—"

Louie stepped quickly between them. "Sh-h-h. Cool it! Jesus, suppose Mom finds out?"

"Your mom's right here and is certainly going to find out what all this ruckus is about." Mrs. Parrish came hurriedly into the room, a frown creasing her forehead. "You're yelling so loud the neighbors can hear."

The three of them were grounded into silence. Suddenly Roz spoke up: "Mom, Marge and I are leaving."

"Leaving? You mean you are going back this time of night?"

"Yes."

Roz watched her mother turn to search the faces of the others. "What's happened here?"

"Nothing, Mom," Louie answered, going over to refresh his drink.

"Son, you never was much good at lying. What is it, Roz?"

Roz looked back at her, this woman, her mother, who had brought her into the world, cared for her, protected her. Now should she in turn protect *her?* Or tell her and get it over with. Unload all the trepidations—let her know, for if she didn't, the weight would always be heavier in the not-telling.

"Well, daughter?"

"Mom, Marge and I are in love."

The woman's face turned ashen, and for a moment, Roz thought she was going to faint. Quickly, she reached out for her, but her mother seemed to back away.

"Roz, I don't understand—"

"It's simple, Mom. Weren't you and Dad in love?"

"We were man and woman."

Roz's eyes pleaded for understanding. How to tell her—to get *through*—to find a common link for comprehension. "The same thing can happen between two women—like Marge and me."

Her mother's head moved slowly from side to side. "It's against God's laws—"

"*Your* God's laws, Mom—"

"Roz! It isn't *natural.* Didn't I raise you right? Are you sick? Has that—that *white* girl cast some kind of spell over you?"

"I suppose you can call it that, Mom. A spell of love."

"*It isn't love!* It's not *God's* way of love!"

Her mother didn't understand. She didn't want to understand; therefore, she couldn't and wouldn't. Don't belabor it—make the hurt worse. "Don't worry about it, Mom. We're going. I thought perhaps it would work out, bringing Marge home here to meet you and Louie. Like Louie bringing *his* wife home—to family."

"Look, Sis. We'll help you. I know a psychiatrist—"

"I'm not *sick*. Louie. This is what I *want."* Her face pleaded with them for the understanding she did not find. "I'm going—" she said, and turned away from those who had once been hers.

V

When she switched on the light upstairs, she found Marge asleep.

Bending over, she kissed her on the cheek. "Honey, wake up. We're leaving—"

Marge opened her eyes sleepily, frowning questioningly at Roz above her. Then without a word, she got up, knowing. She had gone to sleep on the angry voices whose muted sounds came upstairs like a warning fog. Slowly she began to dress like the other time when *she* had gone home to visit and told *them*.

Roz reached out to embrace her. "I love *you*—"

The heat of Roz's body was warm against her. "We didn't get to christen the bed." A feeble grasp at humor.

"Well, we *did* have dinner—"

Downstairs, there was only her mother standing in bewilderment watching them go. "Bye, Mom—" Roz reached out to kiss her, but the woman seemed to shrink at the gesture. Before she closed the door behind what was once home, she heard the words her mother murmured so softly that they almost appeared not to have been spoken at all. "I wish you hadn't told me—"

Outside, a light snow had begun to fall, whitening the streets with downy flakes. The cold air blew against them sharply, bringing them back to reality. "We'll find a motel close by," Roz said, "and spend the night."

Inside the car with the thoughts tight between them, Marge said gently: "Roz—give them time. Perhaps later—"

Roz said nothing. Her mother's words still surrounded her, echoing against her, imprisoning her. She knew that she would always wonder if she should have told.

A MEETING OF THE SAPPHIC DAUGHTERS

Lettie and Patrice arrived at their small apartment almost at the same time that evening as they rushed home from classes. They quickly ate an instant dinner of hot dogs and canned baked beans, bathed and dressed. By seven p.m., both were ready to leave for the meeting of the Sapphic Daughters.

Patrice was more excited about the occasion than Lettie, mainly because initially, it had all been her idea. Lettie had entertained other thoughts for this Friday night which did not include being with what she was certain would be a gathering of all-white Sapphic Sisters. But Patrice, whom Lettie sometimes affectionately dubbed her Oriole Cookie, had a habit of wanting to attend events for which she had no heart. Like the Gurdjieff lecture and Bartók concert last week at Jefferson University where Patrice was working on her doctorate in American literature with the aid of a fellowship. Esoteric lectures and concerts were all a part of Patrice, who was a growth product of the fifties. She was one of the first to integrate the schools in Alabama, and later, became a recipient of one of the rush of handout scholarships awarded to black students by one of the private predominantly white women's colleges in New England for the purpose of inviting Federal monies. Patrice had been around more whites than blacks. Her whole life's itinerary had been a journey through a non-identifiable cultureless milieu. During this time, she was one of the lucky ones who had few problems, for her physical make-up of a light complexion, proportioned features and curly sandy hair, did not cause much of a panic among those white students who feared only the color of blackness.

With Lettie, it was different, for she halfway straddled another generation. Lettie had attended all-black public schools in Washington, D.C., and completed her college work at Howard University, closing her circle of blackness. Even now, the chain had not been too severed, since she taught political science at a community college in a predominantly black neighborhood. The college had a smattering of white students and a top heavy frosting of white administrators. She knew the whites disliked her, for she made them uncomfortable with her outspokenness.

Even her appearance seemed a threat to them. She wore her mixed gray Afro closely cut to the shape of her round head. The deep, rich ebony darkness of her skin reflected the mystery of her long-lost ancestors in the flowing ancestral heritage of her existence. Her dark flashing eyes could change from softness to a cutting penetration when adversely confronted. She was cynical; she knew the world, people—especially white people. About them, she would bitterly warn Patrice: *I don't care how friendly some of them are, when push comes to shove, they're white first!*

"You've tied that headpiece fifty times," Patrice snapped impatiently, watching her in front of the bureau mirror.

"Mind's someplace else—" Lettie replied shortly, now smoothing the folds of her long African dress.

"What's there to *think* about? We're just going to a meeting to hear Trollope Gaffney. The literature passed out at the college's Women's Center stated that *all* lesbians were welcome to attend."

"Uh-huh. But I'm just wondering how many *black* lesbians will be there besides us?"

Patrice garnered part of the mirror to apply lipstick. "It would be nice to find out, wouldn't it?"

"How can we when they're in the closet?" Lettie retorted.

"Well—so are we!" Patrice exclaimed in exasperation, turning to face her. "Have *we* come out to our colleagues, friends—students?"

"For what? To become ostracized? It's bad enough being looked upon as lepers by whites, let alone blacks. You know how blacks feel about— *bulldaggers.*" Lettie spat out the epithet deliberately.

Patrice shuddered. "I hate that word—"

"So do I. But that's what our people call us," Lettie said, softly. Suddenly a smile broke across her face, like sun chasing a cloud as she took in Patrice's shapely form outlined in a sheer summer dress the color of violets. "You look beautiful—"

"And you look beautifully militant!" Patrice laughed, admiringly.

"I'm letting them know in *front* how I stand."

"Com'on, Angela Davis," Patrice teased, "let's go. The meeting starts at eight."

II

The meeting place of the Sapphic Daughters was on the second floor above a curio shop in a shabby brick building near a battery of dilapidated warehouses. A large, husky woman with a hostile face, dressed in faded denims, stood guard at the door, blocking their entrance.

Lettie purposely lingered behind Patrice, fighting off her natural inclination to simply ignore the woman and brush past her. She heard Patrice ask in her nicest Wellesley demeanor: "Is this where Trollope Gaffney is scheduled to speak?"

The woman gave Patrice a long hard silent stare. Lettie smirked, thinking she was probably wondering if she were a nigger, and if so, where did she get that way of speaking.

"Yeah—" the guard finally grunted.

Deciding that there had been enough time spent on social graces, Lettie took Patrice's arm and forthrightly guided her past the door block. Immediately upon their entrance, they were washed by a shoal of white faces gazing at them from behind cold masks.

The meeting hall was an elongated poorly lighted room bordering on bareness. A makeshift platform was at the front with three straight-backed chairs, a small table with copies of Trollope Gaffney's latest book, and a scratched-up podium. Decorating the wall behind was a large cardboard sign reading *Sapphic Daughters* with the interlocking Sapphic symbol beneath. Metal folding chairs had been placed in the center of the room. Along the right wall were two card tables pushed together, covered with white paper cloths for serving refreshments. A large tin tub housed chunks of ice-sheltered beer.

Some of the women were seated, while others milled around in clover group clusters. "Br-r-r, I can feel the chill already," Lettie murmured, looking around.

"Don't be so negative. You just got here. Let's sit in the back row."

"No, indeedy! I've had enough back seat sitting in *my* lifetime!" Lettie retorted. "Front and center—"

The women seated in the fourth row they entered shifted their legs slightly to let them in. One attempted a weak smile. "I don't see *one* of us here—" Lettie observed.

"Sh-h-h—" Patrice hushed her. "I think they're getting ready to start."

Three pants-clad women strode stiffly down the aisle to the platform, feet grinding hard on the wooden floor. "That's Trollope Gaffney—" Patrice whispered excitedly, "in the center."

"How could I miss her?" Lettie retorted sarcastically, watching the little group's important accession to the stand. "She wears the same kind of clothes all the time."

Trollope Gaffney was a tall, broomstick-formed woman with a hard, brittle face reflecting her forties. She was dressed in her usual attire as seen in the newspapers and on the covers of her books: tight sequined brown pants, braided shirt with a gold women's pendant embroidered on the breast pocket, and a beret. The two women flanking her were flushed with pleasure and excitement. One was young with a cupid face dotted with two splotches of rouge, and long brown hair. The other was older, tall as Trollope and had a surly self-important air about her.

Trollope Gaffney sat down first, cocking one leg halfway over the other, then the girl followed. The third woman stationed herself behind the podium, scowling darkly at the women who had not broken their cloistered groups to be seated.

"Please take your seats—" the woman commanded. "We want to start on time."

The groups obediently broke up as the women scattered to find empty chairs. Then the mistress of ceremony called the meeting of Sapphic Daughters to order. Before starting the program, she wanted to remind them about next Friday's potluck supper at someone named Cynthia's house; called for more volunteers to get the Sapphic Daughters' magazine out; and told them that dues had to be paid by the end of the month. Then turning to the girl behind her, she said proudly: "To begin our program, Wendy is going to read us her latest poem which is dedicated to Trollope Gaffney."

There was a smattering of light applause and a barely audible groan from the back. Wendy stood up nervously, taking a sheaf of papers from her bag. In a young, breathy intonation, she began a rapturous reading of her poem:

> She is what I love
> She with her soft beauty
>   who can delight me to ecstasy
> Take! me away on a cloud of
> Woman-an-ly lo-o-ve

"Sounds like the shit I used to write in junior high school," Lettie murmured.

Patrice gave her a warning glance, thankful that the seat directly beside them weren't occupied. Lettie was pragmatic, a realist. She had found this out on their first meeting when they had served together on a Black Feminist panel. They had talked after the discussion, talked into the following months, and talked until they discovered each other and how they felt.

When the girl sat down, there was another polite sound of applause. The mistress of ceremony told Wendy her poem was beautiful, so tender, full of love, such as only women can have for each other. Afterwards, she began reading from a stack of publicity releases to introduce the guest speaker for the evening, Trollope Gaffney.

" . . . one of our foremost lesbian/feminist writers. A leader, fighter—"

When she finally finished, the hall resounded with loud, appreciative handclaps for Trollope Gaffney. When Trollope got up, the room was stilled with attentive, respectful silence.

Trollope Gaffney had a high-pitched voice that derided her aggressive, bold mannish appearance. She was self-assured and spoke without notes, having done this so many times before. Her talk was about the gay liberation movement, where it stood now and projections of how it would be in the future. She envisioned a world community of lesbians. "We have to assert ourselves—*build*. Identify ourselves to each other—this great army of lesbian women, because we are *all* sisters-s-s. We are all *one* in the beauty of Sapphic love-e-e!"

Later when she finished, the hall's walls rocked with cheers as the women stood up. The Sapphic Sisters began crowding the platform to enclose Trollope Gaffney in a web of reverence. The young poet, Wendy, began selling Trollope's book, as the purchasers waited patiently for autographed copies. A record player was turned on, and the nasal voices of a lesbian group singing sad ballads of women in love with women saturated the hall in a plaintive, hollow sound.

"You want a beer?" Patrice asked, let down by the cynical look naked on Lettie's face.

"Now, what was all of *that* speech about?"

"About love and building a world community of lesbians," Patrice answered, as they approached the refreshment table.

"Who needs one? If I'm going to build a separate community of *any* kind, it'll be a *black* one!"

"How much is the beer?" Patrice asked the chubby girl with yellow bangs behind the table.

"Seventy-five cents for a beer, and fifty cents for a sandwich. We got baloney, cheese, tuna fish—"

"Wham!" Lettie breathed. "They must be already starting to finance that lesbian community."

"Two beers, please—" Patrice ordered, searching her purse.

The woman on the platform, who had taken charge of the program, came towards them in long, swaggering strides. "I'm J. L., president of the Sapphic Daughters." Her eyes were a sharp, glittering steel blue, like a frosty, clear winter's sky. She stood back on her legs, hands hooked over her belt, face closed.

"I'm Patrice and this is Lettie—" Patrice smiled, while Lettie eyed her cautiously.

"You live around here?" J. L. asked.

"Yes—" Lettie said quickly, taking the can of beer Patrice offered to her. She had played this scene years ago, many times before, going to places where colored, Negroes, niggers weren't wanted. J.L's question was a familiar conversation piece that dripped with subtle warning. Blacks who "lived around here" knew better than to go to places where they were not wanted.

"Hi!" The girl who had read her poetry came up to stand beside Lettie. "I'm Wendy—"

"Yes, we know—the poet," Patrice said. "This is Lettie and I'm Patrice." Wendy stuck out an eager hand. "We've never had any black lesbians here before—"

"Oh?" Lettie said icily, raising the beer can to her mouth.

"We meet every other Friday. Sometimes we have rap sessions, consciousness-raising groups, and dances—"

"Do you people have any kind of an organization?" J. L. questioned, taking a cigarette from a crumpled pack in her shirt pocket.

"Frankly, we don't know any black lesbians," Patrice said, frowning.

"*Or, if we do, they haven't told us,*" Lettie added, smiling venom.

"Do you know any?" Patrice said to J. L. She swallowed her beer hurriedly. This was a habit with her, to drink beer quickly before it got too warm and tasted like glue.

"Naw—" J. L. squinted over the cigarette smoke.

Suddenly out of a murky past, Patrice was reminded of the red-necked hill crackers in Alabama. Revulsion shivered her spine. After all the transplanted years, she was surprised that she could still remember. Painful memories are never easy to forget, like being hurt in love.

Women began drifting over to the table. A rock group record had replaced the melancholy singers, and a few couples had started to dance. Beer cans were opened and sizzling, popping sounds interspersed with laughter.

"What brought you here tonight?" J. L. went on persistently.

"A couple of things. Primarily, we wanted to hear Trollope Gaffney. I have assigned some of her writings to my students—" Lettie replied, feeling anger warm inside her. *Maybe what really brought her here was the devil to knock hell out of the bitch.*

"And we wanted to meet others like ourselves—" Patrice added, gently.

Wendy edged closer to Lettie, gazing approvingly at her. "That's a lovely African dress—"

"Like *yourselves?*" The words were thrown like acid by J. L.

You goddam racist! Lettie thought, as the beer churned sourly in her stomach. Beer and anger don't mix. White racists and black militants don't mix, and white lesbians and black lesbians are white and black people first, instilled with personal backgrounds of distrust and hostilities.

Seeing the smoldering fire in Lettie's eyes, J. L. backed away, putting out the cigarette in an ash tray on the edge of the table. "Uh—well—you see, this is a kind of *private* organization." She conjured up a weak grin which became a clown's grimace. "We meet at each other's houses sometimes and we are all—er—*friends.*"

"Here comes Trollope—" Wendy interrupted.

Trollope joined them, still surrounded by her network of admirers. "I'm thirsty!" she giggled shrilly.

Someone quickly produced a can of beer for her. Over the can, her eyes glistened at Patrice and Lettie. "And who are *you* two?"

Patrice repeated the introductions, watching Wendy openly gazing at Lettie from beneath heavily lidded speculative eyes. For a flashing moment, jealousy singed her. *Yes, white girl, she's good in bed to me.* Angrily, she finished her beer, throwing the can in a wastebasket.

"We have your last book—" Lettie told Trollope.

"How nice. What did you think of it?"

Patrice held her breath, waiting for Lettie's reply. She knew from long ago how Lettie could raise her husky voice and let it all come out like thunder and lightning in a brass band. Only this time, Lettie was constrained.

"The section on political freedom for women was well-taken, but there doesn't seem to be anything in any of the lesbian literature on the lesbian movement addressing itself to helping the black lesbian to become free from racism—especially *inside* the lesbian community."

Trollope looked puzzled at first, then flustered.

"Will there be freedom from racism in your lesbian world community?" Lettie went on pointedly.

"Of course—" Trollope answered stiffly, looking over and beyond them.

"I had a black lover once—" Wendy blurted out.

J. L. shot her a mean look.

"It's easy to be liberal between the sheets—" Lettie said too sweetly.

Trollope let out a squeal. "There's Tommie! I haven't seen her in ages!" Moving away, she smiled broadly. "Nice meeting you—Patrice and Lettie."

J. L. grabbed Wendy's hand. "Com'on—let's dance."

Wendy waved back to them as she let J. L. lead her to the dancing circle. "Come again!"

"Got enough?" Lettie asked, deliberately putting her half finished beer can on the table. She hated beer.

"Un-huh!"

"Then—let's go."

They left and no one said goodbye.

III

In the bed, Lettie asked sleepily: "Now, has your curiosity been satisfied about the Sapphic Daughters, my little Oriole Cookie?"

"Umph!" Patrice grunted tiredly. "It was like crashing the DAR—"

"Maybe someday, we might find that silent legion of black lesbians. But until then—"

"We stay in the closet," Patrice mumbled, moving closer to her. "It *would* be nice to know—others."

"Perhaps we do. And, possibly one of these days, they'll let us know," Lettie said. "Let's go to sleep. You never know what tomorrow will bring."

HOLLY CRAFT ISN'T GAY

It was four a.m. and Holly had just sunk wearily into the custom-made king-sized waterbed when the phone mocked her. Upon hearing its sound, she groaned. Her body was worn out from performing to a capacity crowd at Town Hall. Immediately following, there had been a late champagne supper distended with false gaiety to hide her fatigue, a brief appearance on the Tomorrow Show, and finally, home to bed. Now, the phone. Victor was probably calling from Washington to find out about the show. New husbands could be a bother sometimes.

She let the phone ring two more times before reaching out from beneath the white satin comforter to turn on the table lamp and stop its incessant pealing. "Hello," she said to an ominous silence meeting her over the wire. Frowning, she pushed herself higher on the pillows. "Hello—" she repeated louder this time.

"Hi, babee-e-e."

The too familiar husky female voice startled her into full wakefulness. It couldn't be! She gripped the red and gold princess phone tightly, not saying anything, afraid to, waiting.

"Babee-e-e, it's *me!*"

There was only one person in her life who called her baby in that slow, seductive way. "Adrienne!" The name came out in a gasp.

"Holly, you *haven't* forgotten. I'm glad, for I would have been *terribly* disappointed coming all the way from LA for your concert. You were marvelous and beautiful to watch. Your voice is getting better and better all the time. I predicted you'd be another Nancy Wilson someday. Remember? That was a long time ago."

A long time ago. Yes, when she sang in small supper clubs and on the road with the Garland Trio. They traveled mostly a tri-city circuit, sleeping in cheap motels, eating Kentucky fried chicken and Macdonald hamburgers.

"How did you get my number?" she asked, hearing Adrienne laugh low. She recognized the laugh—the one meaning that Adrienne, if she wanted, could get and find out anything, including unlisted telephone numbers.

"Simple. Roscoe gave it to me. He was *delighted* to know I came for the big moment in your career. A surprise, I told him."

Roscoe, of course, *he* would. Adrienne could always twist her pianist around her little finger. Why not? Roscoe was pliant and a fag whom Adrienne used to flatter and compassionately listen to about his numerous love affairs.

"Well, Holly, how's marriage life? Are you still a starry-eyed bride after six months?"

"Marriage life is fine, Adrienne," she replied carefully.

"You really picked one, baby. Victor Crowder, Civil Righteous savior of the race. Is he there?"

"No. He's out of town. A meeting with a Senate committee."

"Too bad. I wanted to meet him to discover what *he* had that *I* didn't. Respectability in a *legal* union, I suppose."

She had to cut this conversation off. Get rid of her. Adrienne couldn't come back into her life *now*. She was that part to forget, keep as contained and secretive as possible. "Adrienne, it's late and—"

"I want to see you before I leave," Adrienne interrupted abruptly.

Holly paused, taking a deep breath. Victor was due home in a day. Adrienne Smythe *couldn't* come back. She was a married woman living in the straight world. The whispers had been squelched.

"You usually get up around noon. See, I still recall your habits. Does he wake you up like I used to do?"

"Adrienne—" she began hurriedly, trying to stop the scarlet flush of memories, "how about meeting me somewhere?"

"Oh? I'm not being invited over to see the fabulous house that was featured in *Ebony* last month?"

"No—no, it isn't that—" she protested quickly.

"Sure, I understand," Adrienne replied, like she understood too well. "You can meet me at my hotel."

"What about having lunch?" Holly suggested instead. Lunch would be better than being closed up in a hotel room with Adrienne where no one else would be around to strengthen her against the woman's magnetism.

"The *hotel*, baby, at two p.m.," Adrienne said firmly. "I'm at the Karltz, room 1664. OK? Now, go to sleep. I want my baby looking good for me. Nite, nite."

The phone went dead. Slowly she replaced the receiver, wondering why did the past always eventually find you—sometime? Especially that part she wanted to obliterate. She was safely married to a man who was considered one of the most promising young black leaders heading a civil rights organization. As a husband, he fulfilled the model role of an attentive and loving spouse. In line with this, she complemented his image, giving him the ornamental window dressing of herself, an attractive sultry black star-singer. And he helped her by showing that she had married a man of her own color who was idolized by all. When they made public appearances together, they were singled out as the perfect couple.

Turning off the light, she slid back under the covers and closed her eyes to sleep fitfully until noon.

II

She dressed modestly in a blue pantsuit covered by a tan all-weather coat. Meticulously she tied a scarf around her head and put on a pair of dark glasses. She didn't drive her Mercedes, but called a cab. The day was a typical Big Apple bleak and cold, representing February's dung. While gazing out the cab's window, she wondered about Adrienne. Had she changed much? She had always occupied a corner of her mind, the furtive, dark niche that never came to light, yet was always there.

Adrienne, eleven years older, had taken her under her wing. A nineteen-year-old singer who didn't even know how to dress or wear her hair, but whose voice in the church choir had everybody a-mening on Sundays. Adrienne became the manager for the Garland Trio. She booked them for clubs, special appearances, and kept a watchful eye on the money, and soon, Holly. She had found herself drawn to the outgoing buxom woman with the flat-featured handsome mustard colored face painted with splotches of fire-red rouge and lipstick.

She had to concede that Adrienne could wheel and deal in more ways than one. Before she realized it, she had come to depend more on Adrienne than she realized. What songs she sang best, how to get them over, what to wear, and how to gently put the grasping males back in place.

Even in her personal life, Adrienne became entrenched. She listened solicitously to her problems about the church-oriented mother who didn't want her daughter singing in nightclubs where people got drunk and carried on, and her father, who believed all singers were whores. After a particularly long, drawn-out Saturday morning family hassle, she moved out and in with Adrienne.

Emotional dependability developed slowly, step by step, inch by inch into the physical. The brief female hugs of joy, fleeting hello and good-bye kisses—all part of woman to woman's natural relationship—merged into something else. Living together and sharing brought them closer as one. She ignored the outside warnings about Adrienne from the older ones who frequented the places where she sang. *She's a great gal, but, you know, she's funny.* To her, Adrienne was simply and unequivocally the center of her young life.

The night the friendship became something else was when her mother died. A heart attack in the white home which she worked so hard to keep spotless. The lengthy, tiresome funeral was congested with white uniformed members of the stewardess board, of which her mother was a member, standing like Amazons at the back of the church, while the minister delivered a prolonged eulogy ending with the choir singing her mother's favorite hymns. She sat on the front row surrounded with the white family and her weeping father who had suddenly turned into an old gray man.

Adrienne helped her through it all, comforting her, and that night in the sanctity of Adrienne's apartment, she cried a waterfall of tears. Adrienne put her arms around her, drew her close and pressed her into the warm, pendulous mountain of her bosom, soothing the tears with brief, short kisses that suddenly became one long involved tongue seeking one.

"Babie-e-e, don't cry—" Adrienne had whispered consolingly.

She had closed her eyes to the anxious face of the woman kissing her, astonished at her body's quickening response to the feel of another woman's body heating hers. Then when the husky voice asked quietly if she had done this before, she shook her head negatively, afraid to trust herself to speak aloud. "You'll like it, I promise—" Adrienne had said between kisses assailing her face and neck. "I'm going to give you a warm bath, then we'll go to bed—together."

The taxi driver's gravel voice dissolved her reflections. "Here you are, lady, the Karltz."

The hotel loomed huge and ostentatious above the busy street. When she leaned closer to pay him, his gray eyes stared hard at her from beneath his cap. "Say, lady, you know you look like Holly Craft—the singer."

"Do I?" she smiled, getting out. Not even the glasses and scarf could completely hide a face that had been on the covers of magazines. She walked through the revolving door into the lobby. Somewhat nervously, she pressed the button for the elevator that would take her up to the sixteenth floor and Adrienne.

A smiling Adrienne greeted her in the doorway. To Holly, she looked good, more polished. A mixed-gray Afro made a huge fan above a face holding age well. Only a few faint lines crinkled her eyes, and she had lost weight. By the expensive red lounging outfit she wore, along with the flashing diamond rings and watch, it was obvious that she was doing all right.

Adrienne reached out to hug a reluctant Holly who remained stiff in the embrace. "Ge-e-e, baby, it's *good* to see you!" Suddenly, she laughed. "Why the disguise? Here, take off those silly glasses and the ridiculous scarf. I want to look into those pretty eyes."

"It's good to see you too," Holly said politely, while submissively letting Adrienne remove her scarf and glasses. Adrienne paused to scan her face before taking her coat and hanging it in the closet. She went over to sit on the couch. A table had been rolled in with a bottle of champagne nestled in a bucket of ice and an assortment of sandwiches, cheese and shrimp.

"All the things you like—" Adrienne said softly, going over to the table. Expertly, she opened the wine and poured it into a glass. "Here, like we used to drink it—"

Holly took the glass, not wanting her to bring it up. She wanted to forget all of it. She sipped the bubbly liquid and handed the glass back to Adrienne who sat down close beside her.

With her eyes large and bright upon her, Adrienne drank from the part where the lipstick glaze was. "Well, you're really *the* star now. You look matured—*beautiful.* That body, I see, is more fabulous than ever." Her eyes moved sensuously down over her and Holly knew the old hot weakness brought on by the look. She inched further away to the corner of the sofa. Adrienne's gaze derided her as she did.

"What are you doing now?" Holly asked, feebly attempting to change the subject, for just to hear Adrienne talking to her in that intimately private way could unsettle her. Adrienne could make her feel sexier by merely talking that talk than he could loving. Like the time she came home dead tired to stretch out on the bed, and Adrienne lying beside her had said in that low provocative way: "I'm not going to touch you. I just want to talk to you, relax you—" Though exhausted from the singing, cigarette smoke, alcohol fumes, and greedy male eyes stripping her on stage, Adrienne's voice was like an aphrodisiac pouring a melted, fiery liquid over her. Mesmerized on the soft cloud of the mind-flooding words, she rolled over to submerge herself into Adrienne—to bring love unto love.

"I'm still doing what I've always done. Promoting singers and musicians. Only, I'm more expert at it now."

Yes, that was what had ended it. Bernie Goldman, forty years old and wise, entered her life. The Jewish promoter was adept at making singers. Realizing the potential in Holly, he proceeded to deliberately disintegrate

their relationship both business and otherwise. He told her that he was
in love with her, constantly reminding her that she was a woman and a
woman needed a man. He wanted to get her "out of the life." How could
she know she didn't want a man unless she tried it once? Besides, he
could put her on top, name in lights and print. Finally, under the heavy
pressuring which made her life at home with Adrienne intolerable because
of the jealous arguments, she succumbed and left Adrienne for him. With
Bernie, she didn't feel like a woman but a woman whose body had been
used. This part of her relationship with him she broke off in a week.
There were no more intimacies for she couldn't bear his flabby, florid
face above her or his thickset body pounding into the groove of her.

The business part of the relationship she kept, and he did make her
in the manner promised. He promoted her with a vengeance, always
parading her in the public's eye with notoriously famous and arrogant
black stud male escorts to help project her as a sex symbol. A gay, black
female singer would never make it. The public wanted their black women
stars worshipped, loved and fucked only by men.

But she sang to women and not to the gaping males. She crooned to
the soft hidden faces of the women who could understand what she was
singing about—them—mired in their sorrows, happiness, secrets, loves.
She wanted to touch them with her music, words, make them aware of
their woman—*ness*. Woman singing to women—soul to soul.

"Baby—are you happy?" Adrienne asked gently, untying her thoughts.

Happy? She used to be happy with *her*. The Sundays off of going to
the movies, eating popcorn, and going back home to Adrienne's special
spaghetti and wine, and last, the bed loving until Monday morning. That
was happiness.

Adrienne did not wait for an answer but went on: "Do you have a
lover?"

"My goodness!" She pretended shock.

"What's so outrageous about having a lover?"

"I'm *married*," she snapped back.

"More reason why you should," Adrienne chuckled.

"My husband is my lover—" she said, getting up to go over to the
table for food. The wine Adrienne had kept passing to her was taking
hold of an empty stomach. She selected a turkey sandwich to nibble on.

"How does he love you?"

"What does it matter?" she flared back.

"To *me,* a great deal. I haven't found anyone else I feel the same
about. Have *you?*"

Holly poured champagne into a stemmed crystal glass that hadn't
been used. Bulldykes. So confident—assured. Characteristic of the one

in the audience who watched her like a hawk all evening. White—rich—
at the front table, lowering her lids suggestively over the rim of her glass
which never seemed to leave her smirking mouth. Somehow the woman
had gained access to her dressing room to wait for her after the show.
Later, she found that the entry was secured through a hundred dollar bill.

The woman was seated complacently on a chair, smoking a thin brown
cigar. "My sweet, dusky doll," she had said, "I can tell you're like *me*. I
can recognize the signs in *all* of them." Then the woman moved across the
room to make her pass and she slapped her hard, hissing in rage: *"I'm not
like that!"*

The woman didn't get angry, only amused. "I've *heard* you were. That's
all right," she shrugged, "if you don't want *me*. But you'll *always* go back
to it. Mark my words!"

She had gone back to it, even before rebuking the woman. The urge
to have a woman almost stifled her following Adrienne. It was there and
she couldn't throw off the need. Going to bed with the male studs escorts
didn't help, only made the desire worse. She fought against looking at
women, seeing them the way she wanted to know and be with them. Then,
one night the desire was overwhelmingly strong in her, paining her groin.
She got drunk and went to a gay bar, praying no one would recognize
her. There she let a white dyke pick her up and take her home. The dyke
must have thought she was sex-starved for it had been so long. Subsequent-
ly, she went back infrequently to furtively cruise the bar and be picked
up by a woman. When she scaled higher the ladder of success and moved
to New York permanently, she learned to harness the urge by closing her
mind to it and saturating herself in work. She couldn't afford a mistake.
To keep from yielding to a slip, she married Victor a month after she had
met him where singing for a benefit performance in behalf of his organization in Chicago. The press and public went wild with excitement.

Adrienne came over to stand behind her. The heat from her body
cracked like electricity between them. "I've often thought about you—us.
When I read about your concert, I had to come. To see you in your
triumph that years ago we hadn't dreamed would happen. I'm glad for
you, baby."

"Thanks—" A piece of the sandwich seemed to lodge in her throat.
Quickly she washed it down with the drink.

Adrienne moved beside her to pick at the food. "You really didn't
want to see me, did you?"

"I'm *happy* to see you—"

"Yeah, I can see it bursting out all over you. Don't worry, I won't
let your secret out. You go on and stay hidden in the closet and think
of your career. Me, I'm out. *Way* out now! Everybody knows. So what?

Times are changing. You are what you are and that's it. I feel better. I'm no longer all tight, scared and pent up inside like you obviously are. Even with a husband," she added sardonically.

"I'm not *gay,* Adrienne. The time with you was—well—just a part of growing up."

Adrienne's eyebrows lifted mockingly. "*Six* years for growing up?"

Holly looked away at the shadows darkening the room and down at her watch. "I have to go. I'm expecting Victor to call about what time to pick him up at the airport tomorrow."

"Victor—" Adrienne said slowly. "Don't worry about *him* now, baby." Then Adrienne's arms went around her from behind as her lips stroked the back of her neck. A shiver went over her and she became angry at herself. Adrienne felt her tremble and that was all she needed to know.

"Turn around, baby. Look at me—"

"No—" If she did, that would be all. She had no defense against the memories of how good it used to be, how she missed it with him, and how much she wanted it again with Adrienne.

"Then, I'll look at you!" Adrienne said, quickly stepping around in front of her.

Suddenly she was in Adrienne's arms, returning her kisses hungrily, unashamedly, pressing herself deep into her soft, love heated body. She found it hard to breathe, the weakness in her legs causing her to go lax in Adrienne's arms. She moaned and whimpered until Adrienne murmured into her opened mouth: "Baby, you know I don't like to make love standing up. Let's go to bed."

IV

Afterwards in bed, skin next to skin cradled in Adrienne's arms, she went to sleep. When she awakened, it was past seven o'clock. Adrienne was awake, lying silently beside her, watching her sleep. Seeing her eyes open to mirror her, Adrienne asked: "Think he's called?"

Holly shook her head. She didn't want to think of him at this time. Not while here, comfortably satiated with Adrienne's loving. "When are you going back to LA?"

"In the morning—"

Holly already knew a sense of loss, like a sunflower fading into the evening's dusk. "I want to stay here—all night—with you."

"Be my guest," Adrienne laughed happily.

At that time, she moved to snuggle closer to the woman whom she had known and loved throughout the years. She would never get Adrienne out of her system, mind or heart. She was stuck there in the core of her being.

But no one was going to say that she was queer. She *wasn't* gay. Then the idea struck her. As soon as he got back, she would get pregnant. That would show the world she was a woman in love with her man. By having a baby, no one could whisper or surmise about her. Straight people were hung up on women having babies. Queers can't have babies. A baby would complete the picture of a straight family circle.

While her thoughts planned, she pushed closer and closer into the woman's body next to her own. "Let's not waste anymore precious moments—" she breathed to her woman-lover.

Meanwhile trembling spasmodically to Adrienne's skillful fingers caressing her body, she promised herself that this would be the last time . . . the last time . . . the last time.

ONE MORE SATURDAY NIGHT AROUND

At exactly 6:00 p.m., Marcia drove onto the freeway, joining the Saturday weekend traffic fleeing the city. The heavy torpid warmth of the June evening's air blew against her through the open window, lifting the dark tendrils of her hair into unruly stripes across her face. Here she was again, she thought, hurrying into another one of those Saturday nights. A night with Bethany, causing it to be separate and distinct from the others.

As she drove, her eyes took in the square brick houses skirting the highway. Men, dressed in colorful shorts, sprinkled manicured lawns, while children in miniature images, ran and played and splashed in small round inflated rubber pools. Bethany had children. She had seen their wallet-sized pictures proudly displayed. The last time, one of the children had kept her away. Would the same thing happen again this time? The reminder of the terrifying loneliness of waiting and waiting created a sheet of mirrored fear within her. She remembered enduring the long hours alone in the motel room, until the phone rang and Bethany told her that one of the children had gotten sick at the last minute and she couldn't come.

A horn blew, startling her attention back to the road. A truck rumbled past like a snorting bull, leaving a trail of noise and diesel fumes. Her small sports car trembled and swayed as the monster roared by. Once, when Bethany was riding with her at a time just like now, Bethany had gripped the seat and asked in a small weak voice: "Why don't you buy a larger car like mine?"

"Why would I need a station wagon for just mother and me?" she had replied, laughing, while mentally counting Bethany's family of three, leaving out *him*.

The speedometer inched upwards as she drove faster. Each minute of *this* Saturday night was precious. If Bethany, by some good fortune, were already there, then time had been wasted. But somehow, she knew she wasn't there. It took her longer to get away. Sometimes it was a miracle that she could get away at all.

Finally after what appeared to be a longer time than it was, she saw the exit sign reading Greenbriar. At last! She was almost there. She eased her speed to turn off to the ramp. A cluster of filling stations greeted her at the mouth of the strip checkered with beckoning hamburger stands, fried chicken carry-outs, the Ten-Foot Drink Bar, and Ling Fu's Chinese House. Restless cars and people, mostly young, roved aimlessly, exploring the summer night.

Their motel was off from the main thoroughfare, protected by trees and woodsy seclusion. She parked in front of the office and went in. The same man as a month before was behind the desk. He was thin and old and uncaring. His bland face showed no expression as she filled out the registration form and he handed her a key.

She went back to the car, a little flushed, knowing her real reason for being there. She could never get accustomed to motel trysts. She would have preferred her own place, but this couldn't be. She got back in the car and drove around to the back where the room was assigned. There were few cars in sight. It was still light. The spaces would fill up later.

II

This was the longest and hardest part of all the Saturday nights such as this one: the anxious and solitary waiting. She never knew exactly when Bethany would arrive. It all depended upon how long it took her to get away from *them*—if she could.

To occupy the time and fill up her thoughts, she began the mechanical motions of unpacking her overnight bag and hanging up her clothes. First she took out the green slacks and yellow blouse, and then the dress her mother always insisted that she take on her "business trips." To have one would be on the safe side in case of need, she advised, for after all, wasn't Marcia the head of Marcia Thompson's Women's Marketing Consultants? Lastly, she opened the cosmetic case which bared the bones of her beauty: eyeshadow, lipstick, powder, rouge, fingernail polish, comb, and brush.

What she needed was a drink. Instead, she reached for a cigarette. She would wait and share that initial pleasure with Bethany. She sat down in one of the hard modern chairs by the window, and looked around at the room similar to all the other rooms purporting to be a home away from home. The bed appeared burdened with its heavy spread, and the cream-colored walls loomed more comfortless with thoughtlessly placed pictures. Despite its prosaic appearance, Bethany and she preferred this place because it wasn't too near or too far away. It scored points above the others. Anyway, they only needed a room.

Wanting more light, she partially opened the drapes. The evening was dying slowly. The moon was out high and full and regal. She could see the lake behind the motel through the stalwart line of trees. A speeding motor boat sliced the waters with the grating noise of a buzz saw. This was the worst part of the Saturday nights—the waiting. Questions crowded her thoughts. Was she able to get away? Had there been an accident? Bethany was a careful driver. She was careful about everything—even long ago before she met *him*. She was the one who made double-certain that no one saw her come to the dormitory room, the door was securely locked, and shades drawn. Bethany was so guardedly safe that no one suspected the whole of their four years in college. Bethany dated males and kept her secret life with Marcia stored away in a private place. Then graduation— the parting—and the end for them.

The end until last year when the class of '64 had a ten year reunion. Then they came face to face again to discover they lived in neighboring towns only one hour apart. Thus the Saturday nights began—exquisite in reuniting the lost and found, making togetherness again.

Impatiently she put out the cigarette and got up to move restlessly about the room. If Bethany didn't hurry and come, they wouldn't have time for dinner. There was too little time. She turned on the TV. The Saturday night movie was on. A western. The sounds of galloping horses and gunshots filled the room. She stretched out on the bed, closing her mind to the sounds and waited.

III

The ringing jarred her awake. It was Bethany in a telephone booth. She would be there in a few minutes. The trembling of her hand revealed her excitement. Happiness and relief flooded her. Bethany was on the way!

After a while, the knock came softly. At first, because of the TV, she didn't hear it. Then it came again louder, and the familiar voice called to her.

"Marcia—it's Bethany."

Springing up, she smoothed back her tousled hair and hurriedly unbolted the door to Bethany smiling at her. Bethany was shorter than she, and Marcia could see over the top of her head. Again, whenever she looked at her, she thought of what the years had done. Bethany's body was rounder, almost plump now, and well-defined lines threaded the small mouth curved in a not-outstandingly attractive face. Time can mark changes as it had with herself. Marcia looked at her in the dimness and knew the heat of the sun without its rays.

"Darling—" she drew Bethany inside as the door swallowed the space behind her.

"Getting away was something else!" Bethany exclaimed in exasperation. "The babysitter was late, and little Bobbie wanted ice cream when there wasn't any. And his father couldn't find—" she stopped abruptly, throwing Marcia a "I'm sorry" look. *His* name was never mentioned between them. Although *he* existed, they pretended that *he* didn't, even though the specter of *his* presence was always there—dark, silent, intruding upon them. You couldn't completely close out that which was defiantly real.

"I'm starved. Let's eat at the place where we got the delicious seafood the last time," Bethany suggested.

Marcia frowned, trying to remember. The last time had been four weeks ago. It *had* seemed longer.

"It's about three miles down the lake drive—" Bethany helped out.

"Oh, yes. I remember. All right."

Bethany tiptoed to kiss her lightly. "And let's hurry back!"

"Yes—let's do!" Hurry back to the only home they knew together.

IV

After the first loving, which was quick and excitable, they went back to sleep: Bethany with her buttocks pressing into the curve of Marcia's hips, knees folded, closing the flower that Marcia had made bloom. Awakening to the softness of Bethany pressed into her caused heat to spring life into her loins. Once again, the beginning waves of need, longing, and desire nudged her like an impatient but gentle brook.

The soft strands of Bethany's hair in her nostrils made a ticklish sensation of wanting to sneeze. She inhaled its freshness, as if it had just been washed for her. She made herself stay very still, not wanting yet to awaken her, to interrupt the deep contented sounds of her breathing— satisfied nuances of after-love. She could always satisfy her. Could *he* make her moan in abandonment, grip *him* tightly, moan and cry and laugh with shameless pleasure?

Outside, over the low monotonous drone of the air conditioner, she could hear the mating call of a cricket. For a moment, she was sad, listening to the male summoning his female. She had no chirping song. The sounds of car motors grinding to an end, doors slamming, male voices intertwining with their women's high pitches, sifted through her ears like gravel. Bethany did not stir.

Gently, Marcia reached to cup one global mound of her breasts—pliant full softness which overflowed like a too-abundant cloud in the palm of her hand. She moved her fingers delicately as if caressing the wind. She knew sadness. Their moment in time was drawing closer to an end. It was getting late. They never had enough time. Stolen time is never enough.

The cone covered by her hand was set in motion as Bethany moved, murmuring in her sleep. Was it her name she had drawn into existence or someone else's? Her heart quickened as her hand crept lower to lay flat leaves of fingers across the hill of Bethany's stomach. From the other side of the wall, she could hear the low muffled sounds of the television in the next room. A door slammed in the corridor outside. Why did there have to be intrusions in their sanctuary of love?

Bethany murmured again, obliterating the foreign sounds. It *was* her name. She knew happiness. Bethany stretched awake, and Marcia's fingers on her stomach floated with the movement. Turning, she smiled at Marcia and the smile was fuller than the moon outside. Then Bethany leaned to kiss her lips. Marcia could taste love. Her hand quickened to caress her back and linger on the dimples above each buttock. She pulled her closer and closer, submerging, wallowing, entombing her body in the softness of Bethany. It was this softness she craved.

"What time is it?" Bethany whispered in the cavern of her neck.

Marcia lifted an arm free to look at the illuminated dial of her watch. "Ten—"

"We still have time—"

Marcia sighed. Time. There was never enough. "Do you want to—once more?"

"Always. Once more."

The point of Marcia's tongue began to weave wet-tipped patterns everywhere. In its wake, savoring powder, perfume, lotion and dew from the love-making gone before.

In one sensuous slow, almost motionless movement, like a butterfly lasciviously spreading its wings, Bethany stretched out on her back and waited. Marcia felt glowing, warmly excited as the desire to love and be loved inflamed her. She rose above Bethany, burying her head between the cleavage of her breasts, while her hand created a windstorm in her hair, lifting, smoothing, catching the strands between her fingers.

"God—I'm glad that I found you again—" Marcia said, words warm in the spot where her lips were.

"Me—too—you."

"I remember how we once were—"

"Now, much better. We're older!" Bethany laughed a tight laugh, for with Marcia's kisses touching her here and there, the smoldering sensation within her thwarted laughter. "Marcia—" she managed to whisper against the tumult of her emotions.

"Hum-m-m?"

"I've never been like this with anyone else. Have you?"

Marcia was silent. She believed her. She knew not like *this*. She felt Bethany shift beneath her to look directly into her face. "Do you believe me?"

Did she detect panic? "Yes—of course, I believe you." She wanted to close out why she believed her. Long ago, even when it had first started, Bethany was uneasy about the liaison. It was her courage and will and patience that had held them together. Away from her, it was less difficult to accept the way which did not call for strength.

"And you—have you?" Bethany's words scissored her thoughts.

Why had she asked? Why must beds be turned into confessionals. Ten years can bleed for a lot of living. For her, there had been others *and* others like her. How was she to know that she would find her again? Life had to be lived. Moments go on. People must go on and try to love. She knew Bethany had understood the answer which did not come.

Then quickly, as if she had not prodded, Bethany said: "I'm glad we found each other again."

Marcia's arms tightened around her to obstruct the thoughts that did not belong here in this place with them. Her mouth moved to Bethany's— heat to flame. She felt her breasts combining with Bethany's, twins entwining together. Her hand moved below, smoothed, stroked where the love-ache was, until Bethany gave a little sigh. Marcia's arms tightened around her, pressing her body down down down until bottom lips kissed together. The side of Bethany's face warmed her cheek. There had been no one else who could make her feel exactly like this—fine, luminous, ethereal.

The flames of love and loving fired her. But above the ecstasy of her own emotions, she, the lover, thought first about the one she loved. Separating her ardor, she made herself hear Bethany's cries of pleasure and endearments engulfing her name. Marcia was happy, knowing it was she and what she was doing that gave Bethany the joy of her feelings. Then, deep within herself, she began to feel the tremor, the familiar ache that shot sharp spears through her. Trembling, her hands reached down to slip beneath and pillow the swaying of Bethany's hips, guiding the rhythm of her movements.

In the back of her mind, she wondered again if *he* could do this to her too. Suddenly as the passion between them rose to reach its highest sensation, Bethany arched herself to glue them tighter together. Then, the piercing sweet-pain caught them both and made two one in the pinnacle of love.

The burning moments were over, but still, Marcia held her close to her until Bethany's breath was no longer a gushing fountain. The storm was ended. They both felt free. Free?

Later, when the edge of feeling was less sharp, Bethany asked: "Is there anymore wine?"

"I think so. A little." Marcia moved to get up.

"No—stay. I'll get it."

The lamp became an encroacher as Bethany snapped its brightness on. She followed the sight of Bethany's nakedness crossing the room to the dresser where the light white wine was—once chilled, now warm. A momento from their dinner. She wished that she had let her get it for her.

The bed sank when Bethany returned with one glass for two. "Take some—"

Marcia sipped it. The liquid didn't taste as sweet as she. Lighting a cigarette, she drew upon it, then put it to Bethany's lips. Bethany inhaled deeply and made the embers glow. Marcia could no longer hear the television in the next room. When was it turned off? While in the heart of love? Suddenly the sounds of a bed took its place, squeaking an intimate tell-tale pattern. She was glad theirs had not.

"I have to go—" Bethany said softly, putting out the cigarette.

Marcia thought: she always had to go by twelve o'clock. Like Cinderella, would she turn into a pumpkin? Sometimes, she wished that she would. Then she would have her forever. She took a deep breath, forcing the words into steadiness against the thought of her leaving. "Be careful—driving back." Fear afterwards, kept her awake like a ceaseless headache during the night.

"I'll be all right."

Bethany bent down to kiss her lightly. Marcia closed her eyes. She didn't want to watch her get up, prepare for departure—leave. Her heart turned into itself. She could hear the bathroom noises—toilet flushing, running water, silence. Marcia opened her eyes when Bethany returned, wearing the blue dress she had forgotten to tell her was pretty. Now she was prepared to go back to her real world—home to *him* and *them*. Bethany poised over the bed, a slight abstract frown clouding her face. Both feigned bravery.

"I'll try to call you. Tomorrow night—" Bethany said.

Marcia knew she would, providing that she could. If *he* were there, she would have to wait until another time. Bethany looked down at her so long that it seemed the earth had stood still. The earth had not. It was only they.

Bethany left, closing the door behind her and that which had been the two of them together. Marcia listened to the sounds of Bethany's car. She could tell it above all the others. She had heard it many times before in this place and others like it—transient rooms crowded with off-shaded secrets. The car was the last sounds of her leaving.

Now loneliness made itself known. The stark barrenness of the room mocked her as prickly thoughts needled her. How long would this last? Always she wondered if this parting would unknowingly be the end. She realized that Bethany would never leave *him*—the children—the house. In these were safety, security, sanctioned by the world's highest blessing. Another might, but not Bethany who lacked the strength to leave.

But if crumbs were all she would have, then crumbs she would take. It had always been Bethany, and always would be. In the morning, she would get up and leave to go home where someone waited for her too. A someone who would not be understanding or sympathetic to such as they. The silence was deafening in its loneliness. She thought about her again and knew that this would be all she had until when and if she saw her again. She would have to wait until another Saturday night came around.

A BIRTHDAY REMEMBERED

"Hello—Aunt El—?"

The familiar voice came over the telephone, young, vivacious, excited—a girlish echo reminding her of the past. "Tobie—"

"Happy birthday!"

"Thank you—" Ellen felt a rush of warmth, pleased that Tobie had remembered. But hadn't Tobie always. Besides, her birthday wasn't difficult to remember, falling on Valentine's Day. *A heart born especially for me,* Jackie used to tease.

"May I come over?"

Now Tobie's voice sounded a little strained. Ellen could visualize the puckers of thin lines forming between her wide-spaced eyes. The tightness in her throat delayed an answer. Why shouldn't she? Then again, why *should* she really want to? Tobie no longer belonged to her—*them*. When Jackie died a year ago, Tobie had to go back to her father. A splintering separation, after all their years of living together, *belonging* together—Tobie, Jackie and herself.

The three of them had survived through the tumultuous stress of trying to make it, ever since Jackie walked out on Roger and came to live with her. Tobie was just five years old—too small and pale for her age, too nervous from the parental arguments.

Roger had been furious, appalled and angry at his wife's leaving him for a woman. Ellen knew it was more an affront to his male ego than losing Jackie. Particularly when it belonged to one who was striving ruthlessly to become a top business executive, amassing along the way all the exterior garnishments that were supposed to go along with it. He had purchased a large, two-story brick colonial house in the suburbs, replete with swimming pool and a paneled country squire station wagon for Jackie to do her errands. When she left him, he had tried to declare her temporarily insane.

Ellen thought that perhaps Jackie *had* been crazy to leave all of that and come to live with her in a cramped apartment on her salary. She wasn't making that much at the time as a staff writer for *Women's Homemaking* magazine's food section. But, somehow, they had made out, until Jackie got a job teaching in an elementary school. Jackie loved children, and had a way with them.

"Hey—Aunt El. You still with me?"

Tobie was waiting for an answer. One could get so involved in the past. "Of course, dear. Please *do* come over," she invited, thinking it wasn't until later she was to have dinner with Harriet. All she had to do was change from her jumpsuit to a dress.

"I'm bringing a friend who I want you to meet. Ok?"

Tobie never had an abundance of friends, only special ones who were close, for that was her way. At first, she and Jackie had mistakenly thought Tobie was ashamed of their relationship—what they were to each other. They knew Tobie was aware of it. How could she not have been. Real love can't be hidden. It inevitably is transmitted through a glance, affectionate touch, strong feelings that show.

Then there was the rainy, cold night in November, one month after Jackie had left him, when Roger came to the apartment, hurling threats, shouting obscenities. He was going to take them to court, declare them perverts, unfit to raise a child. Tobie must have heard the words flung out at them through the paper-thin walls.

"Wonderful, darling. I'll look forward to meeting your—friend."

The phone clicked and Tobie wasn't there anymore. Ellen remained seated on the couch, motionless, as if the remembrance of all that had gone by in ten years had risen like a mist to cover her in sadness. There had not been a divorce because of his man-stubbornness and Jackie's woman-fear for Tobie. When she died, he buried her. She hadn't been allowed to do this one last thing for Jackie. To *be* with her during the last rituals, to hold a fourteen-year-old who was in all but flesh, her daughter too. The next morning after the funeral, Tobie came by to be with her, to cry her tears, sustain her grief. The sorrow shared as one was their solitary entombment for her. Through the passing days, the biting cruelty of it all slowly healed, leaving only the scar tissue. Jackie had been laid to rest in her heart.

Ellen's eyes fell on the array of birthday cards on the coffee table and the vase of red roses that Harriet had sent. Meeting Harriet had helped her to get over the travail of death's cruel separation. Incurable illnesses are like earthquakes—they swallow quickly. It wasn't too bad now. She could look back and recall without too much pain. All it takes is someone to help, someone who cares, and the eraser of time.

The living room was beginning to become shaded with dark-fingered lances of shadows. She reached over and turned on a table lamp. The day was quickly vanishing into the grayness of night. What she should do was get a drink. A good, stiff celebrating birthday martini. After all, she was forty-four years old. Six more years, if still alive, she would reach the half century mark.

She got up and went to the kitchen. There she turned on the light which brought into sharp, garish focus the ultra-modern bright chrome and copper, resembling the spacious kitchens featured in her magazine articles where various culinary talents were exhibited. Thankfully, through her writing skills, she had been able to help make their living better before Jackie passed. She had become editor of the food section and had written a cookbook. Her publisher had assured her that cookbooks always sell, and hers had.

A martini called for gin, vermouth, lemon, and an olive. She got out the glass pitcher and stirrer. Jackie preferred sunrises. She made them for her in the evenings, after the lengthy daily struggles of climbing the ladder together. Jackie had become principal of the school, a model for those beneath her, and an in-school parent for the students. Ellen marveled at how she had blossomed, learning to become independent after being a college trained housewife to Roger. *There's so much to living that I did not know before,* Jackie had told her happily. Yes, indeed, there was a lot to living that neither had known before.

She mixed the drink in the shaker, stirred it slowly and poured some in a glass, topping it with a round green olive with a small red eye-circle. *Here's to you, Ellen Simms, on your birthday!* She lifted the glass in a toast and the drink went down smoothly. Then the doorbell rang. Tobie must have been just around the corner. As soon as she responded, Tobie sang out cheerfully: "Happy birthday to you—happy birthday to you!"

Tobie hugged her and Ellen found her nose pressed into the cold leather of her jacket. Tobie seemed taller. *They do grow,* she mockingly reminded herself, comparing her own short stockiness to Tobie's height.

"A present for you, Aunt El—"

When Tobie thrust the gift into her arms, Ellen protested: "You shouldn't have." The package was neatly store wrapped and tied with a pink ribbon holding a card.

"You know I never forget your birthday, Aunt El—"

At that moment, she saw the boy standing awkwardly behind her. He had a round, friendly face and a mass of dark brown hair parted on the side.

"Hello—" she spoke to him.

"Aunt El—this is Warrick."

"Come in and take off your coats. Would you like some hot cocoa to warm you up? I know it's cold outside." Tobie used to love hot cocoa with a marshmallow floating like a full-grown moon on top. This was her favorite on Sunday mornings when they had a leisurely breakfast together.

"Cocoa—you *know* what I like!" Tobie exclaimed, throwing off her coat and curling up on the sofa.

Ellen watched her, noting the girlishness hadn't gone yet in the transitional adolescent stage. She looked older. Her blonde hair was cut short and bangs covered her forehead. Physically, she looked more like her father with the sharp, angular face, but there was her mother where it counted most, in her warmth and quickness of smile. Did her father know that she was here—with her. Like visiting a widowed parent—eight years of child-rearing, child-caring, child-loving.

"Open your present, Aunt El—"

"All right." First she read the heart shaped card with the fringed edges about Valentine birthdays, and then the scribbled message: *To my one and only, Aunt El, with love, always.* She blinked back the tears and made a fanfare out of unwrapping the gift. It was a big, glossy, illustrated, expensive cookbook of ancient Eastern recipes.

"Thank you, my dear." She leaned over to kiss Tobie's cheek. "It's lovely."

"Tobie saved up a week's salary to buy it—" Warrick announced proudly, settling in the rocker opposite the sofa. His voice was changing, and there was an inflamed red pimple beside his nose. On the front of his red and white pullover sweater were the words Terrence Academy. The right sleeve had a large white T.

"Warrick! Shame on you giving my secrets away," Tobie laughed, playfully chastising him.

"Where are you working?" Ellen asked, hanging their coats in the closet. She couldn't imagine Roger Ewing permitting his teen-aged daughter to work.

"I'm a library page after school at the branch near home. I like to have my *own* money—" she added reflectively.

Ellen hesitated, wondering if she should ask. Don't forget the social amenities. Isn't that what they had taught Tobie throughout the years. "How is your—father?" she asked, the words sounding like cracked dry ice.

"Oh, Dad's ok," she shrugged, kicking off the high wooden wedge platforms with interlacing straps. "His main object in life seems to be to prove how much money he can make and *keep.*"

Roger's a miser at heart; he wants every cent I spend accounted for, yet he'll go out and buy something outlandishly showy to prove he's got money, Jackie had commented about him.

Why was it that people happen to be in certain places at the right or wrong time? Like the dinner party she had been assigned to write up for the magazine to describe the elegance of the food, drinks and table setting. There seated next to her was Jackie, looking small, frail and lost among the spirited laughter and inane chitchat of the moneyed. Roger was on her other side, appearing to be thoroughly enjoying himself talking to the big bosomed woman with the glittering necklace and frosted white hair. There was the interest at first sight, hidden hormones clashing while a subtle intuitive knowingness flashed hidden messages above the clamor of the room. *If only we could decide our own fates, what would life then be?*

"I'll make the cocoa—" she said, retreating to the kitchen.

The martini pitcher was on the counter where she had left it. Immediately she poured another drink. She had been ruminating too much. Stop the past. Drink and be merry. Chase the haunting memories away.

"Aunt El—need any help?"

Tobie came in. She had put her shoes back on and they made a hard noise against the linoleum. The wedges looked like ancient ships, causing her to wonder if they were comfortable. The bell-bottom blue jeans billowed over them like sails. "No—nothing to making cocoa. After all the times of doing it for you—" The reminder slipped out. She wished it hadn't.

Tobie laughed, and the sound made everything all right again. "What do you think of Warrick?" she asked, reaching into the closet for cups and saucers. Everything was known to her in a place that had once been home.

"He seems like a nice—boy." Suppose it had been a girl? People choose who they want. This they had tried to instill in her in their unobtrusive way. "How does your father like him?"

"Dad hasn't met him yet," Tobie said quietly. "I wanted to get *your* opinion *first.* Anyway, Dad stays busy and away so much that we don't have much time to talk. The housekeeper takes care of the house—and me—who, I suppose, goes with the house." She gazed down at the floor, biting her lip, face clouded. "I miss Mom—don't you?"

"Yes—" she replied softly. "But we have to get used to living without loved ones. That time must inevitably come, sooner or later, for somebody."

She turned away, pretending to search the refrigerator so Tobie couldn't see her face. Do something else while waiting for the milk to warm. Prepare sandwiches. Young people were always hungry—feeding growth. She had cold chicken and potato salad left over from last night.

"I thought if *you* liked Warrick, Mom would too. He plays on the basketball team," Tobie continued, watching her slice the chicken and take out the jars of pickles and mustard from the refrigerator.

"Are you—serious, about him?" Ellen asked, praying that she wasn't. Not at this stage of youth—almost fifteen.

"Of course not! We're just friends. He's someone to go places and do things with."

"Good!" Ellen exclaimed, feeling an impending burden lifted. "There's plenty of time for the other. You have to go to college and—" she went on hurriedly about those things which normally fall in place for young lives.

Tobie smiled. "I *knew* you were going to say that, Aunt El." Then she looked directly at her, blue eyes locking Ellen's in a vise. "Anyway, someday, if I ever *do* get serious about someone, I hope it will be as wonderful and beautiful as what you and Mom had together."

God, for the first time, it was out in the open! She felt the shock of the words, unexpected, frank—a blessing. "I do too, dear. Like we had." Her hands trembled from the weight of the moment between them. A bridge had transformed Tobie from girl to woman now to her.

"Aunt El, the milk's boiling over!"

"I've lost my cocoa-making expertise," Ellen laughed, snatching the pan off the burner. The milk had boiled into a bubbling white-coated cascade of foam.

When the tray of food was ready, they went back to the living room where Warrick was watching TV. While they ate hungrily, Ellen finished her drink, feeling light, warm and happy.

When the telephone rang, it was like a rude interruption into a special cradle of time. Harriet wanted to know if she would be ready around seven-thirty for dinner. She glanced at her watch. It was just six o'clock. Besides, what was more important to her than this?

Later, Tobie said: "We'd better be going. Warrick's taking me to the movies. Thanks for the treat, Aunt El."

"And, thank *you* for the present. I'm glad you came by to make my birthday a happy one. *Both* of you."

"Nice meeting you, Miss Simms," Warrick said, extending his hand. "Tobie talks about you all the time. Now I can see why!"

She liked him. "Come back—anytime."

Tobie kissed her goodbye at the door. When they left, the tears were finally freed—in sadness and happiness too. Tobie was going to make it all right. Jackie would have been proud. They had made good parents.

LOVE MOTION

"Can't you mo-o-o-ve?" he hissed in her ear.

Saturday night and he was a familiar hulking dark shadow above her, a pantomimist executing the sex ritual of time—the movement of centuries which started with what and who and how? Satur—*day*. Relaxation for *him*—her husband—doing nothing—something: washing the car, out with the dudes/drinking, coming home early for a home screw if nothing was giving it up on the outside. Home to no sweat for you know it's there and betta- -be-e-e—rea-a-a-d-dy!

Saturdays and she was tired and worn out with the cleaning, shopping, washing, ironing. She thought of tomorrow—the day of rest—which would be no better: preparing the children for Sunday School, cooking a bigger meal for company.

Nicie felt him begin again: in and out and out and *in*. It was like the children's song accompanying a game of entangled arms—go in and out the window. Her window was dry and his meat felt like a blunted sword in the open cavity of her. The bedsprings squeaked in mousy protest. Could the children hear? Perhaps those strolling past to escape the night heat of the summer streets could hear below the love motions and giggle: "Somebody's sure gittin' it on-n-n!"

He positioned himself better upon his knees, arms slanting, imprisoning each side of her shoulders. She saw his backsides comically humping up and down and thought of the fresh sheets—ruined.

"*Move*, goddamnit! How you expect me to *feel* anything? I can't get turned on with you lying there like a mummy!"

Turned on—get soul in your ass. Turn *him* on. Turn yourself on. To turn on herself, she had to go into herself, her thoughts, her mind's eye of the inward vision—the imagination. She, herself, Nicie, into dreams, fantasies. Which one would she choose *this* time from her accumulated repertoire of the streets, sights, daily encounters? Who would be her phantom lover?

Her thoughts drifted away, beyond the grotesque realism of him—dismissing him—the man-raper charging into her, invading the richness of her being. Fly away on a visionary cloud. Get a savior.

Where?

The one on the bus last week when she was coming home from work. She had noticed her as soon as she got on—the long, slim lines of her legs beneath the colorful, flared cotton skirt, and the soft, rounded globes of her breasts showing through a sheer summer blouse, pillows upheld by a white-laced brassiere. As the woman searched for a seat, their eyes met and held. A magnet: the woman sat down beside her. Graceful fingers with red-tipped puddles held closely a large yellow straw pocketbook with a round orange sun in the center. She felt the warm softness of the woman's hip accidentally pressing against hers with the jerking motions of the bus. She had repressed the urge to reach over and touch her—this woman who smelled deliciously of perfume and powder.

The smell of him above her was of stale cigarette smoke, sweat, and the scotch he had been drinking all day. The remembered odor of perfume and powder of woman came back, haunting her, filling her. She let her mind inhale it, feeling the freshness creep down down down into her like the clear air of a new rain-sprayed morning. Powder and perfume spelled woman which was good—good—good.

"You feelin' it now, huh? Old man's got you goin—"

She recalled how hard it was to keep from touching the woman on the bus. To reach out and *feel* her face, arms, thighs. She had kept her neck painfully turned and strained to stare out the window at the street scenes. Once, she relieved the tension of her neck turn and gaze at the smooth contour of her face—the color of cinnamon, cheekbones high, full lips painted the color of her nails. As if she knew of the interest, the woman turned with a lined sketch of a frown on her face that slowly flitted into a faint smile. She swallowed hard. A sharp stirring routed her groin, which released a wet secretion between her legs.

She trembled at the overwhelming desire to embrace her. She had never held or been held by a woman. Never been *loved* by a woman. What would it be like? To feel, press, knead, kiss, stroke, and fondle a smooth, female body like her own? To *know* herself physically through the arms and kisses and tongue of another woman—an image of herself?

Would it be like this, now with him, whom she was trying to erase. Nicie closed her eyes tightly to transform him into the *her* on the bus. Magically the body above her became warm and soft and smelled of perfume and powder. Lips pressed against her own, identifying, matching, opening slightly to connect tongue to tongue, offering and giving of self and promises as hands made covering laces of cobwebs over her body. Fingers sought and covered her breasts, cupping them into a warm soft glove, heating them like a stove. She moaned.

"Humph!" he grunted, moving faster.

Now her hands reached up to grasp her phantom woman-lover's head, to lose her fingers in the hair that was softer than the crisp hair below. Her woman-lover's head moved to kiss kiss kiss down down down in circling wet teasing patterns on to where the looping middle button was imprinted in her stomach. She gasped, pulling the face back up to meet the savage bite of her kiss and taste the light salty traces of herself. And as she did, the hand went down to fan, caress, part, find and touch the occult wonderment of her.

"God, baby, you're gittin' *hot!*"

Obliterate *him.* Think of her—the *woman* above her, the woman loving her, the woman who in other faces and forms came to rescue her from *him.* She moved so *that* part of her could feel. The woman's mouth kissed her bottom lips as her breath blew ether in a hot draft of flames into her.

Oh, Jesus-s-s, now! She almost whispered aloud to her woman-giver. *Go down on me.* Her mind woman-lover's lips rested above the crown of her glory. *Please, don't tease.* Then, slowly, her phantom lover buried her face into the life of her and made her live again.

"Ugh!" Release came for him.

He pulled out of her to flop like a dead fish over on his back. When did, on her mountain of cloud, it came for her on the tip of a tongue of soft sweet burning fire. "Ah-h-h-h!"

His face turned to the side to look questioningly at her as she curled in a fetal knot and moaned. "What the hell is the matter with *you?*"

What was the matter with her? Nothing except it was *fantastic!* Her eyes were closed. Her lover had gone, but the delicate traces of the love-pain remained inside her. Phantom woman—gone—back into the cage of her dreams, the still life of her mind. Maybe someday, she would get a real one to love of perfume and powder and woman.

A SPECIAL EVENING

Saturday—why did it have to rain? Toni thought, gazing out the water-smeared windows. March was so unpredictable. The morning had been bright and clear, but in the afternoon, the sky's glaze grew shrouded with warning signs. Still, despite the threatening clouds, she held to the hope that the somberness would eventually lift.

In the evening, after seeing the last patient in her office and going home to bathe and dress, the rain came. There was a crash of thunder, the switchblade flash of lightning, and the rain descended in a torrent of swift heavy release.

A week of anticipation and preparation for the dinner engagement was now marred by ugly weather. An evening she had looked forward to and planned for with such carefulness. It should have been beautiful with silver stars and a full benevolent moon christening the sky, for wasn't an evening such as this supposed to be designed by poets? The way Sappho would have made it?

She turned from the window, hoping that Letia wouldn't change her mind. Some women just didn't like to go out in the rain. Another worry to vex her. As yet, the telephone hadn't rung, and it was six p.m. She had better hurry. Letia was expecting her at seven and the drive across town would be slower because of the rain.

In the bedroom, getting her car keys off the bureau, Toni glanced into the mirror. The expensive black tailored pants suit, trimmed with white braid, fitted neatly, camouflaging the slight bulges of late middle age. A hint of natural lipstick was applied just right to the strong mouth, and deft touches of powder gave the broad handsome face a touch of softness. Vanity, she admonished herself—no one was completely without it.

She had collected her keys, annoyed at the way her hands shook, like a teenager's on a first date. Ridiculous. But this was a special night with a special person. She hoped it would go well.

She rang Letia's doorbell exactly on time, in spite of the blinding rain that the windshield wiper could hardly cope with. Letia opened the door and said, with concern: "You're almost drowned!"

"Not quite—" she smiled at Letia, who was wearing a long multi-colored hostess gown that fell in waves over her slim figure down to her ankles. Her thick dark hair was swept up in spiraling tiers above a too-thin pale face. The sight of Letia caused a lonely pearl to form a knot in Toni's throat and turn to stone in her stomach. To conceal the way her eyes had been embracing Letia, Toni said hurriedly and a little fearfully: "You aren't going out in *that*, are you?"

Letia laughed as she closed the door behind them, barring the world. "Of course not! Here, give me that wet coat. You need to dry out. Go over by the fireplace, Toni—" A small question anxiously pocketed her mouth. "You don't mind my calling you Toni, do you? Doctor Reis for office hours."

"No, certainly not, please do. I'd like it very much." She crossed over to the fireplace to focus her gaze on something else—anything except Letia who was hanging her coat and hat in the closet. The apartment was small, tastefully furnished in delicate soft feminine appointments, but functional.

"I thought since it was so messy out we could just stay here and I'd cook something," Letia said from across the room.

Toni turned the suggestion over in her mind. The rain's hoofbeats against the window galloped in tune with her heart. How many times in the short while she had known Letia had she wanted this? Thinking about it alone at home during the nights, after the endless parade of patients who needed healing, consoling, attention. Can a dream distilled suddenly come alive?

At her silence, Letia said quickly: "I *can* cook, you know." A smile's hint covered her lips.

"I believe it," Toni laughed reassuringly. "It's just . . . well . . . wouldn't you prefer going out? After all, I *did* invite *you* to have dinner with me."

"It won't be any bother—cooking for you," Letia said, watching for an approving response.

Toni turned her gaze back to the fireplace to grasp a newly feigned interest in the bright flames. What did she mean? *Cooking for you.* Or had she misinterpreted the meaning? The words caused a shiver to run a fine sharp line through her.

She couldn't afford to misjudge. She had been hurt before. It was so

easy to fashion other peoples' words into meanings you wanted. That was
the trouble with being like she was: it was terribly difficult sometimes to
really know. With some, the signs were apparent—by a glance, gesture, in-
toned word, thought perception. She couldn't afford to make any more
mistakes. She was getting older. She had learned from the mistakes of the
past—only a few—but enough. Enough to have left a bottomless reservoir
of hurt inside her brimming with the painful words: *I'm not like that.*

"Well—" she faced Letia again, "if you don't mind. I'd enjoy having a
good home-cooked meal. I usually eat out. Too tired to cook after work."

"Good!" Letia's face brightened, pleased.

"May I use the phone? I'll have to cancel the reservations."

"It's by the couch. What would you like to drink? Scotch, bourbon?
A martini? I'm an awful drink mixer."

"Scotch on the rocks will be fine," Toni said, going over to the telephone. Perhaps that was what she needed to relieve the tension. She called
the Ledo and cancelled the reservations. Wearily she sat on the sofa near
the wall with the shelves of books. A large desk was opposite her, cluttered
with paper, a typewriter and pencils. This was probably where Letia did
her writing. Children's stories. That was what she had said when she'd
wandered into her office one night suffering from gastritis.

"I write children's stories . . . when I'm well," she had added facetiously.

"Here's your drink—" Letia was back.

Toni thanked her. "Anything I can do?"

"No," a shake of the head. "There really isn't that much to do." She
sat down beside Toni with her drink.

Toni smelled her perfume like roses on a fresh morning. She tasted her
drink. The scotch spread warm tentacles through her.

Letia reached for a cigarette and automatically Toni picked up the
table lighter and flicked it alive. Letia bent to the flame, cupping her
hand lightly around Toni's. She breathed in the smoke, and then blew it
out in a gray wavering stream.

Toni set the lighter back on the table, thinking, now wasn't that
butch? But it was instinctive with her. One of her give-away features, she
concluded wryly.

"It was really lucky for me to have walked into your office that night,"
Letia began conversationally. Then narrowing her eyes thoughtfully: "It
was raining that time too."

"Yes, it was," Toni said softly, also remembering. Was the rain an
omen?

"I was so sick. I was coming from my agent's office, and luckily saw
your office sign. It was very kind of you to look at me when you were
ready to close up. I felt like a fool after I found out you were a noted

surgeon."

"I'm not noted," Toni protested modestly.

"Anyway," Letia smiled, "I'm glad I was sick. I got to meet you." She paused reflectively, flicking ashes in the tray. "I don't know anyone whom I've felt so comfortable with in a long time."

Toni looked across the room. Be careful how you answer, she warned herself, wanting to say one thing, but instead, she said: "I'm glad. I like your company, too."

She thought about the few times in the past two months when they had chatted over the phone. The first time she had called was on the pretense of finding out how Letia was. Afterwards, the calls were mutual ones that consisted of sharing of interests and thoughts, and above all, discovery.

"Do you?" Letia half-turned to face her, drawing her gaze back. Her brown eyes met, held and searched Toni's questioningly.

Toni wondered if she were looking for a sign. "Yes, you know," she went on briskly, "I'm quite fortunate. I have a rapport with most of my patients."

"Patients—" Letia tested the word, while putting out the cigarette. "Am I not a friend too?"

"Certainly," Toni replied softly, raising the glass to her lips. The social helpfulness of a drink. It occupies the hands and elasticizes strain. "I consider you a friend. Didn't I invite you to dinner?" she smiled.

Letia was silent as she sipped her drink. "How long have you been in practice?" she asked abruptly.

"Too long, I'm beginning to think. I'm getting old and tired. I think it's about time for me to fold up and have some fun before I get much older."

"You aren't old—"

"Aren't I? I'm a few years ahead of you," she sighed, running her long fingers through the short black hair sprinkled with silver.

"It's beautiful—" Letia murmured, watching her, "your hair. It looks so soft. Is it?" She touched Toni's hair, her fingers as gentle as a feathery wind. "It is—" she laughed shakily, scattering the fragile moment into a thousand broken pieces.

Toni felt warm icicles pricking her skin. *Please don't touch me again, she cried inwardly, for I won't be able to stand it.*

"Have you been doing any writing lately?" Toni asked, fumbling for normalcy again.

"Uh-huh. I'm finishing a story about a little girl who didn't like Christmas."

"Did you know a little girl who didn't like Christmas?"

"Yes—" Letia's fingers toyed with the purple sash of her gown. "I had

a very close friend once whose little girl didn,'t like much of anything."
Quickly she finished the remains of her drink. "My friend did everything
in the world to get her to like things."

"Did she—finally?"

"No, not until I left. You see, she didn't like me. Thought her not-for-
real Aunt Letia was a threat between her and her mother." Suddenly she
laughed bitterly, not wanting to talk about it anymore. "I'm going to
check on dinner. I don't want you sitting here starving while I bore you
with segments from my past."

"You aren't boring me. I want to know—about you." And she did.

Letia's eyes fastened upon her. "You—what about you?"

"There's nothing to tell about me. Except hard work to get where I
am in a field where males dominate. A double hard road for one to travel
from a poor Minnesota family of five children."

"Any special friends?" Letia asked quietly.

Toni ran her thumb up and down the sides of her glass. A question
harmless to many, but for her, one that could trap, ensnare—betray.

"Well, did you?" Letia persisted.

"What?" Toni sparred.

"Have any special friends," Letia repeated impatiently.

"It depends on what you mean by special. Friends are special for
special reasons."

Frowning, Letia got up suddenly. "How do you like your steak?"

"Medium."

Letia gathered the empty glasses, signs of not enough or too much.
"Would you like to watch TV or listen to some music?"

"Tonight, I'd rather have music," Toni said, looking up and seeing the
frown still there. The fine lines between her wide-spaced eyes were almost
permanent now. She would have liked to erase each with a kiss. But can
one erase time?

"What do you like? I have an assortment. Pops, blues, show tunes,
symphonies, jazz," she announced gaily, waving her hand in a mountainous
brush. "Which?" Then, without waiting for an answer, she pulled out an
album. "You look too pensive tonight. I'll put on some jazz. This is Jonah
Jones. I like his style."

She placed the record on the turntable and the muted trumpet of Jonah
Jones softly assailed the room. Toni leaned back, giving up her thoughts
to the music. It was then she began to feel tired, drowsy. The patient load
had been heavy for the day, and the suspense of tonight had added to the
strain. She closed her eyes.

Something cold touched her hand, startling her. She had almost fallen
asleep, and Letia was standing above her holding a fresh drink.

"Here's another one to wake you up. Dinner won't be long."

"Thanks—" she grinned sheepishly, accepting the drink. "Guess I'm not used to such carryings on."

"Stick around. It might even get better," Letia retorted saucily. "If you'll excuse me, I'm going back to the galley."

Toni sipped on the drink. It was short on ice and long on scotch. Her thoughts focused on Letia. Was she or wasn't she? Almost like the hair rinse commercial, she smiled to herself. She wanted so much to hold, touch, and caress her. Say the things she wanted to say. Males had no problems such as she. By role playing, they were the aggressors, and an approach was not an indictment, but something expected if the time, place, and moment were right. With her, a direct approach could be quicksand. There was so much to lose.

The drink was making her more sluggish, too musing. She stood up and stretched. Perhaps she should offer to help again. After all, she *was* to have treated Letia to dinner.

She heard the rain vying with the music, drumming steadily against the window.

Toni decided to take her drink and go through the door where Letia had gone. Letia had an apron on now and was standing on a stool reaching into the cabinet. Not hearing Toni behind her she backed down and bumped against her.

"Oh!" she gave a gasp of surprise as Toni's arm instantly reached out to steady her. A little of Toni's drink spilled on her suit.

"I'm sorry," Toni apologized quickly. "I thought you heard me come in."

Her arm was still around a startled Letia who was loosely holding a forgotten wooden salad bowl, and suddenly she was aware of Letia's face so near and the warmth of Letia's body. She dropped her arm limply to her side.

Letia stayed in the circle, invisible now, that Toni's arm had once made. The warmth of her breath lightly touched Toni's chin as she stared up at her intensely. There was a smudge of flour on the tip of Letia's nose, and Toni wanted to wipe it off with a kiss she did not give.

"Next time, doctor, rattle your scalpels," Letia laughed shakily.

"I'll remember," Toni promised, backing away. "I just wanted to know if I could help with anything—" And be with you.

"No, thanks. I have the operation well under control."

Letia busied herself at the sink, breaking crisp lettuce into the bowl. Toni found herself staring at her—the way her head tilted to the side, the slight slump of the small shoulders, her concentration on the task before her. A rend like a sharp ache seared through her. She wanted so much to brush her fingers across Letia's face, to know, trace and remember. And last, to cup her chin in the palm of her hand and lock her eyes with hers.

She would have to wait until she was sure, and sometimes one was never sure.

Outside the rain's sounds had grown softer, sounds of slow diminishing. Jonah Jones' *Cherry Pink and Apple Blossom White* surfed the apartment in a misty musical spray.

"I'm glad it rained," Letia said, slicing tomatoes over the lettuce. "I like it here better with just the two of us."

"I like it too—" The words escaped before she could stop them and form others. She became aware that she was still holding her glass. The ice had melted and the drink was warm. Politely she finished it and set the glass on the sink.

"If you really want to be useful," Letia said, "fix two more drinks. The liquor's in the buffet in the dinette. You might as well learn where I keep it."

"All right." Toni picked up their glasses and went into the dinette off the side of the kitchen. A round table was covered with a white linen cloth and glistening silverware. Two bronze candle holders in the center flanked a floral piece. It looked intimately inviting. She got out the scotch and carefully measured out two jiggers each.

"Get some ice out of the refrig—" Letia directed when she returned.

Toni filled the glasses with ice cubes and watched as Letia slid two thick red steaks under the broiler. She handed Letia her drink, fingers brushing her, and quickly withdrew her hand as if from fire. Letia cast her a quizzical look, then smiled: "Here's to — us."

She lifted her glass in the toast, feeling a little tight already. Not real high, but nice and mellow and happy. Watching Letia bending over the steaks, she suddenly felt hungry.

Her gaze swallowed Letia's movements and came to rest on the small cleft in the back of her neck where lips could fit. A glow began to spread warmly through her. She could wait, for wasn't waiting and wishing and hoping the vine of life—in the life?

THE MISTRESS AND THE SLAVE GIRL

Heather sat uncomfortably in the stifling heat of the carriage. It was April, and already the heavy southern sun dominated the sky. Sighing wearily, she lifted her layer of skirts slightly above her ankles to fan her legs. She could hardly wait to get home, take off her clothes and twist her hair off her neck. The humid air didn't seem to bother her brother, Ralph, dozing beside her. Probably nothing would, since he was fortified with whiskey.

When George slowed down the horses, she frowned. They were passing the crowded slave market. She disliked having to drive by, but it was on the way back to the plantation. The throng of bargaining, narrow-eyed men, and pathetic sights of the Negroes sickened her. George must dislike it more, for he too was in bondage. Since the age of thirteen, he had been the carriage driver. Now his hair was almost white.

After her father passed six months ago, she had to come back to Virginia. More liberal minded towards women and slaves than most of the surrounding planters, he sent her to be educated in the north. Years of being away had made her virtually a foreigner to this place where she was born. In a pleading letter, their family lawyer had beseeched her to return, or the plantation would have to be put up for sale because of mismanagement. There was no one else to take over, for her mother had died giving birth to Ralph, a year younger than she, twenty years ago.

Ralph had no interest in business matters, which was evident at the cotton mill this morning. Possessing a literary bent, he stood out like an abolitionist in the south, where there were more slave masters than poets. She was the one with the mind of steel. Watching him nodding, she could see some of herself. Both had burnt-auburn hair, reedy bodies and somber faces. Her features were more refined than his, and skin paler. She had her mother's light gray eyes; whereas his were darker with a pit of sadness in them. He displayed a kind of weak handsomeness, sporting long sideburns and a thin moustache above a sloping mouth.

The carriage came to a standstill as George was forced to stop for the flesh buyers blocking the way. Impatiently, Heather leaned to tell him to run over them if necessary, so they could continue on. As she did, she saw the young slave girl on the auction block. The girl was very pretty with cream colored skin and long black wavy hair falling down her back. Standing stiffly erect before the gaping men, she stared vacantly over their heads, as if looking into another sky. The black suited auctioneer was frowning, while whispering in her ear. No doubt, he was admonishing her for not smiling, Heather surmised.

"A likely wench," the auctioneer began. "Seventeen years old. Healthy. Good teeth. A fine one for the house!" A smirk crossed his face.

"One thousand—" Someone shouted.

"One thousand," the auctioneer echoed. "Do I hear fifteen hundred?"

Something about the slave girl fascinated Heather as she took in the pink silk dress hugging the curves of her body. She knew that they dressed the goodlooking ones purposely like that. The sad haunting aura hallowing her only enhanced her beauty. Heather swallowed hard as she experienced a familiar sharp sensation piercing warmly through her.

"Fifteen hundred!" A second bidder.

"Come now, surely she is worth two thousand!" the auctioneer challenged. Abruptly he bared a breast, exposing a perfectly molded mound with a brown tip. "See—" His whip lifted her skirt to shapely legs. "A fine specimen!"

As the men automatically surged closer, Heather thought: *My God, what beasts!* Anger flared within her at the sight. Reaching over, she shook her brother awake. "Ralph, come!" she ordered, climbing hurriedly out of the carriage. "I'm going to buy that girl."

Blinking, Ralph looked at her in astonishment. "My dear sister, I thought you weren't going to purchase any slaves. 'Slavery dishonors the human race,'" he quoted her mockingly.

Pushing through the group, she called out calmly and clearly: "Two thousand!"

The men stared at her in disbelief. Ladies in these parts weren't in the habit of outwardly bidding for slaves. That was a male perogative.

"Twenty-five hundred!" proferred by an oily looking man smoking a cigar.

Heather recognized him as the town's tavern owner with the brothel above. "Three thousand," she advanced.

"Ah-h-h, you're attracted to her too, my sister," Ralph whispered.

"Come now! Four? Do I hear four thousand?" the auctioneer bartered greedily. Hearing no takers, he barked loudly: "Sold to the lady for three thousand dollars!"

"That's Heather Blakely. Got a mind like a man's for business," Heard from the crowd.

Ignoring the undercurrent of comments about her, Heather said: "Ralph, please get her for me."

The transaction settled, Heather got back into the carriage, feeling triumphant as usual when outsmarting males at their own game. This was one slave girl who wouldn't be thrown to the wolves for a white master's breeder or concubine.

"She's up front with George," Ralph informed her. Slumping down into his seat, he took a silver flask from his coat pocket.

In exasperation, she lashed out: "Must you?"

"Yes, *I must!*" he retorted, deliberately taking a healthy swig. "Now, tell me, what do you intend to do with your expensive beauty?"

Perspiration dampened Heather's arm pits and back of her dress. Removing her hat, she fanned her face and neck. "She will work in the house," she responded crisply. The remainder of the ride was in silence.

Washing the road dust from her face, Heather changed into Ralph's riding breeches, her favorite plantation attire. Then she had Beulah, who was George's wife, longtime family cook and surrogate mother, to bring the newly bought slave girl into the library.

As Heather sat behind her father's desk, the girl stood facing her by the window against the fading sun. To Heather, she seemed delicate looking, poised with her hands loosely clasped in front. Like before, Heather was aroused by the sight of her, generated by an overpowering magnetism. Tentacles of desire flamed through her at the place where desire is utmost.

To offset the unsettling stirrings, she looked out the window at the slaves leaving the fields in the twilight to go to their cabins. She was uncomfortable in the girl's presence. This was the first slave she had ever purchased, making her a firsthand slave owner. The idea did not cheer her.

Clearing her throat, she asked: "What is your name?"

"Delia—" The word was barely a sound.

Delia, Heather repeated in her mind, and without a "ma'am" or "mistress" added like the others would have. The girl was definitely not servile in her speech or appearance. An air of dignity emanated from her in the stately way she stood. Heather was reminded of the Negroes with whom she attended the private school in Boston, daughters of free black men, and the southern white slave owners whose consciences pricked them to educate their illegitimate daughters.

"What can you do especially well? I mean—"

"I know what you mean," the girl replied evenly. "I can sew." A hint of haughtiness was in the answer, heightened by the flashing of her dark eyes. Her voice was well-modulated with no trace of the slave dialect.

Heather's eyes lingered on the tilt of her head that made her hair curtain one side of her face. "You're very pretty, Delia," she said, almost in a whisper, surprised that she had spoken her inner thoughts aloud.

The girl gave her a questioning look, brushing her hair back from her face. As she did, Heather saw the dark bruise by her ear. "How did you get that?"

"I was struck by the slave trader."

Heather's mouth tightened. Getting up, she went to her, reaching out a tentative finger to the spot. Immediately she was sorry, for the girl's skin was like velvet, soft, smooth, exciting, triggering want. "I'll never strike you," she said huskily. "Ever."

The girl's eyes softened. "Thank you—" A slight smile curved her mouth, relaxing the rigidity of her body.

Heather looked quickly away, focusing her gaze again out the window. The girl had brought up feelings that she had tried to submerge years ago, only to find now they had come alive once more, stronger than before. She hadn't wanted this to happen anew, not since the unhappy school episode revealed in letters from her lover, which were accidentally discovered by Ralph one Christmas while at home. Close-mouthed, he had said nothing, not even to her about them.

"You'll be my personal servant, Delia. I know you're tired. I'll talk with you in the morning." She heard the girl leave, and only then did she dare to look with hunger in her eyes at the space where she had been.

Ralph, even though intoxicated, managed to make it downstairs to dinner. Beulah's ample form, clothed in a white apron, hovered over him, trying to entice him to eat the ham and rolls she had prepared. Seeing her brother picking at his food, Heather wished that she could persuade him to get away from here, the south with its power for weakening men with artistic strength.

"Beulah, are you getting Delia settled?" she asked, filling her plate with food.

"Yas'sum, Miss Heather. She in the kitchen eatin'."

"What do you think of her?" Surely the girl would be less fearful among her own.

"Well," Beulah's dark face frowned thoughtfully, "she quiet, like she cryin' hard inside 'bout sumpin'. She got soft hands, like she never done no hard work befo'."

"If that's true, Beulah," Ralph broke in, "I'm certain my sister doesn't intend to break her work record. I might even be inspired to write a poem about her. Too bad she doesn't have a brother of comparable beauty."

Heather gave him a silencing look, as Beulah's face assumed the mask of the house slave: see nothing, hear nothing, think nothing. Heather ate pensively, head down, thoughts busy on tomorrow and finding out more about Delia.

The morning's early heat permeated the bedroom where Heather sat at her dressing table. Turning to Delia, she questioned: "Have you cut hair before?" When the girl answered in the negative, Heather handed her a pair of scissors. "Let's give it a try."

As the cut tresses lay scattered on the floor by the chair, Heather scrutinized the effect in the mirror. She resembled Ralph more than ever now without his moustache and sideburns. "It's much cooler this way," she remarked, running her fingers through the short strands. "Don't cut yours," she said, reaching up to finger Delia's hair. When she did, her hand grazed the girl's face. Quickly she drew back, for it was like touching a candle, burning her. For a long moment, the girl's deep black eyes grew darker, appearing to swallow her in their depths. Heather fought not to embrace her, to kiss the sweetness of the face she had felt. The erotic vision made her dizzy with longing.

"I'm going downstairs to breakfast," she said brusquely. The room had become unbearably hot to her.

Ralph was slouched at the dining room table, shirt opened at the collar, eyes red-rimmed, drinking coffee. "So, you've cut your hair," he noted instantly. "Another link to wearing pants and buying a slave girl?" he laughed sourly. "What role are you trying to play, dear sister?"

"I'm *not* playing *any* role," she snapped. "But since you mentioned it, what I would *really* like to be is an abolitionist. Free the slaves, sell the plantation and go back to the north to live."

Ralph shrugged indifferently. "All right by me. Do what you like."

"Then," she added kindly, "you would have enough money to go to Paris and write."

"And not be an oddity among the southern patriarchy," he muttered disparagingly, setting his cup down hard.

Sympathy welled up in her for him. If only he would let her get closer to him. They were two people in the wrong bodies for this age and time. She ate her breakfast hurriedly, then summoned Delia to go for a walk with her. The morning was shaded by an overcast gray sky. Walking with the girl, Heather found she could look down on her, for she came just to the tip of her shoulder. She was sharply aware of her, the quiet breathing that made her breasts rise and fall, and the light footsteps trying to keep up with her long strides.

"Let's sit here for a while," Heather motioned to a large Oak tree where a robin was perched, cocking his inquisitive bright eyes at them. "I used to sneak out here as a child to get away from everybody."

When they dropped to the ground, the robin, sensing his intrusion, blessed them with a chirp and flew away. Leaning back against the tree, Heather asked: "Where did you come from, Delia?" Like a strange being dropped from the sky into her life, she wanted to know more about her, this beautiful girl who affected her senses so much.

"New Orleans."

"Who taught you to sew?"

A shadow grazed the girl's face as eyes downcast, her slender fingers tugged at the grass. "My mother—" She choked on the words, seeming on the verge of tears.

Without thinking, Heather automatically took her hand to comfort her. The hand fitted like a small muff in the palm of her own. "What's troubling you?" Heather questioned gently.

"Nothing—"

"Something *is,* but you aren't going to tell me." She squeezed her hand. "Someday, I hope you will." Thunder rumbled its warning bass in the sky. "We'd better go back," she said regretfully, "before it rains."

The rain stayed with them all day, steady, refreshing, cooling the air. To combat her thoughts of Delia, Heather busied herself with updating the plantation records, filling in expenses, slave births and illnesses. Towards evening, she grew tired, and went to her room to lie down. What she needed was a good book to relax her. She told Delia to go down to the library and get Tennyson's poems for her.

While waiting, she suddenly remembered: slaves weren't supposed to be able to read, only she had never thought of her as a slave. When Delia returned with the book, she said quietly: "You can read."

"Yes." Delia looked hesitantly at Heather, wondering if she should have shared this knowledge. Sensing her mistress's calmness, she continued slowly: "My mother sent me to a free school."

Heather sat up quickly on the side of the bed. "Was she a slave?" She had to have more answers to piece together the puzzling enigma of this girl with whom she was falling in love.

"My mother was *not* a slave," Delia replied firmly, tossing her head back proudly. "She was a free woman."

"Then, *you* were free," Heather stated, aware of free issue. If the mother was free, the child was born free.

"I—I was kidnapped by slave traders when my mother died."

"How horrible! What about your father?"

"He was my mother's master." Her voice lowered. "He set my mother free before I was born. I don't know anything else about him." She began to cry, letting the pent up ordeal of suffering come out into tears.

Heather went to her, holding her closely. "You're going to be all right," she hushed, "here with me. You'll sleep in the alcove off my bedroom. Be here at all times. Close to me."

The girl's sobs subsided in the protective circle of her mistress's arms.

Heather could not sleep, blaming it on the rain, but knowing it was because of Delia. She could hear her tossing restlessly in the bed, as muted sobs escaped from her dreams.

Restraining the urge to go to her, Heather buried her head in the pillow, hugging its softness like a woman's body. Delia's face spun a disturbing vision in her own dreams, the haunted look and mid-night eyes that were beginning to light up at the sight of her. Yearning made a warm cradle in her stomach. She did not fall asleep until daybreak.

The accident occurred in the afternoon. Ralph's horse reared up and plunged wildly across the field, knocking Delia down while she was gathering flowers for Heather. George carried her into the house, followed by a stricken Ralph.

"I'm sorry, Heather," he apologized in the library where Heather was working. "It was a new horse—skittish." His eyes pleaded for forgiveness. "I know how you feel about her. I know."

From the turmoil of her dazed thoughts, she looked up at him sharply. *He knew!* But how could he not? Their blood was the same, their sexual proclivities against the norm. When she stood up shakily, he reached out to hold her comfortingly. A loving warmth bonded them, for adversity can spark a closeness never known before. They empathized with each other, responding to that which at no time had been spoken aloud, but understood between them. Regardless, he was her brother, and she, his sister. Kissing him lightly on the cheek, she fled upstairs to where Beulah was tending Delia.

Upon seeing her worried face, Beulah smiled reassuringly. "She goin' to be jest fine, Miss Heather. Didn't do much. Just scared her to deaf."

Bending over the bed, Heather asked, "Are you all right?" *Dare she touch her forehead? Smooth her hair? Lean closer?*

Delia nodded, smiling, seeming pleased that Heather was there.

"I'm glad." Heather's fingers were lighter than a wind smear over Delia's cheeks.

That night when darkness fell, Heather went to her, a shadow seen moving across the room in the lamp's glow. "Would you like to sleep with me?" She caught her breath in fear, holding it until the answer came. She couldn't order, demand, for it wouldn't be the same.

The girl's face first showed surprise, then a rare happiness blooming in the dimness like a flower opening to the sun. "Yes—" A quiet response that said so much.

The fantasy in Heather's dreams had come true. Together in the large canopy bed, Heather drew her close, basking in the warm curves of Delia's body pressing into her own. An exploratory fingertip traced a lone pattern on Delia's face, pausing at the eyes, narrow nose broadening at the nostrils, and the full sensuous lips.

"My Delia—" Heather breathed hoarsely. "You know, some women can feel about one another the way men and women do."

The girl was still in her arms, head nestled on Heather's breast. Finally, she breathed softly: "I know—now." Tenderly she looked up to cup Heather's face, as if taking a picture with her eyes. When their lips met, it was a fusion of soft petals wet with dew.

Leaving her lips a baby's breath away, Heather asked: "Has anyone kissed you like that before?"

"No—"

Heather felt gladness winging in her heart. Gently she kissed her again, opening the girl's lips with her own to slide her tongue in the chamber of Delia's mouth. Breathing hard, Delia's arms wound tightly around Heather's neck, as she shyly responded to the kiss.

Slowly Heather began to remove Delia's gown. "I want to see your beautiful body." Next, Heather took off her own garment. "Now! I can feel you better against me." Naked they embraced, body to body, warm flesh blending as one.

Lightly, Heather caressed Delia's breasts and round stomach. "You're so fragile, like a jewel. My precious jewel." She kissed her forehead, tasting the saltiness of her skin with the tip of her tongue. The trembling of the girl's body imparted the message she wanted to know. Fired with passion, Heather stroked the tapering thighs inside and out, then stopped between them to fondle where the brushfire was. The wiry pubic hair tickled her palm as a middle finger went into the moist entrance to another wet warm mouth. The girl's legs parted to better receive the instrument pleasuring her. A moan spoke of her ascending emotion.

"Delia, say my name," Heather whispered, nibbling on an earlobe.

"Mistress—"

"No! I'm *not* your mistress," Heather retorted half angrily. "I'm your lover."

"Lover. Heather."

"And you are my love." Withdrawing her hand, Heather bent down below to place a kiss on the small sunken hollow in the middle of Delia's stomach, then trailed her tongue straight from its path to where her hand had been.

She blew a warm breath into the furry patch before sending her tongue on its lascivious journey. Again Delia moaned, clasping her fingers in Heather's short crop of curls.

Suddenly Heather rose from the fountainhead of rapture to cover Delia's body with her own. Gently she improvised a slow sensuous rhythm, sealing bottom lips with ecstasy. Delia's face contorted as sweet agonizing pain swept through her. Like she had been born with the knowledge of this loving, her body moved in perfect harmony to Heather's cadence.

"This is the way I like it," Heather murmured in her ear. "Loving as one. You with me, and I, with you, my wonderful dark princess. I love you!"

"And, I, you!" Delia replied breathlessly.

The heat of sex ignited a tumultuous fire between them, causing an excruciating paroxysm of joy. Simultaneously they came with stabs of blinding goodness overpowering their bodies on a comet of loving.

Months later, Heather freed the slaves and sold the plantation. Ralph went to Paris to live and write, where there was a heritage of those like himself. Heather moved to Boston, taking Delia with her. There they shared a house sheltered by love. No one knew they were lovers, only that the white and black women, who lived together, were terribly devoted to each other.

WOMEN IN A SOUTHERN TIME

Eulah Mae stood over the sink, taking her time about washing the lunch dishes. Occasionally she would look up to gaze out the window at the myriad cluster of spring tulips, roses and azaleas, radiant beneath the balmy southern sky.

The house was quiet, for Miss Tish had taken Miss Monti upstairs to the little parlor opening to the balcony off from her bedroom. "We're going to catch a breeze, Eulah Mae," Miss Tish had smiled back at her as they climbed the winding stairway. Upstairs seemed to be Miss Tish's favorite place whenever Miss Monti came to visit. They would stay up there for hours, just the two of them alone.

Carefully she lifted the plates out of the warm, sudsy water that formed glassy beads against her hands, and placed them in the rack to rinse. She had been working almost a year for Miss Tish, since graduating from high school last June. Upon answering the ad in the paper for a maid, Miss Tish had taken one look at her in the neat Sunday dress, pillbox straw hat and white gloves, dressed proper like her high school counselor had advised, and said that she would do just fine.

She planned to work until enough money was saved to go away to nursing school at Meharry in Nashville. She had long dreamed of becoming a nurse. She liked taking care of people and had frequently helped her mother with ailing friends. She even took care of her mother before she died last winter. She loved the white nurses' uniforms, which imparted glamour to her youthful mind. Now she had on a white one, but covered with a black apron.

Eulah Mae dried the dishes and stacked them in the cabinet beside the sink. She was luckier than most of her friends who worked for white people. Her job wasn't hard, especially after Mr. Southerland went to the army. With him gone, not as many people came to the house. He liked to entertain, particularly his men friends. They would come over anytime of day or night to drink, play poker and tell jokes. Most of all, they complained about the war taking away all the good nigger field hands, and how Roosevelt was mollycoddling the niggers. If their wives were along, the women would chime in, whimpering over the loss of good colored maids and cooks to the ammunition factory in Spring City, twenty miles away. None seemed to heed Eulah Mae's presence serving them.

Only the men would sneak glances at her, admiring the shapely figure showing in the plain uniform. The wholesomeness of youth was enmeshed in her looks, silky smooth cocoa skin, and fresh smell. Her mother used to say that she should smile more, be less serious. But she had always been thoughtful, turned into herself, grave as advancing twilight.

She soon discovered that Miss Tish often retreated from the phalanx of men when they came to visit her husband. She would flee to the outdoors of winding paths and trees, or phone Miss Monti to come over and go for a drive to get a change of scenery. Miss Monti liked to drive that big, gray Packard of hers. Eulah Mae could hear her coming down the road at top speed, careening up the oval to screech to a stop of squealing tires in front of the house.

Miss Monti Irving was different from the rest of the white women in town. She wore her dark hair in a stylish bob, smoked cigarettes in public, wore pants most of the time, and said "damn" whenever the mood struck. Miss Monti ran the local newspaper that had been in her family for years. An only child, she had always been high-spirited and independent. At least that was what Eulah Mae's mother revealed to her during those winter evenings when she ruminated about the town and people engrained into its soil and insulated within its borders. Everybody knew each other, and had grown up in proximity, if nothing else. The whites and blacks were tied together in a web of interdependency—the whites through need and the blacks for survival.

Some whispered that Miss Monti was a Communist because of her unconventional behavior and radical dress. She wanted to put the colored school principal on the town board and bring in industries to inject new blood in an otherwise incestuous town. They laughed her away, saying that she had gotten hold of those notions in college up North, and the right man would come along and simmer her down someday. Miss Monti was thirty-four years old, still without a man, and the same. In a way, she had become more rambunctious since the war, writing editorials in her paper on freedom for people here, too.

The town tried to overlook her bohemian ways, for she was, after all, one of them. Born and bred here, not an outsider. Nor a man. Women could do no harm. They continued to buy her paper despite the editorials, for it carried the social and church news, and grocery store values.

Eulah Mae could see that Mr. Southerland didn't quite like Miss Monti by the way his too handsome movie star's face glared disapprovingly when she came to visit. Of old, pedigreed southern stock without the accompanying money, he lived in his wife's family home and ran her grandfather's canning factory. Perhaps, because of this, he kept a grim-lipped silence during Miss Monti's visits.

Miss Monti seemed good for Miss Tish, who would brighten up like a Christmas tree when she came over. "I swear, Eulah Mae, Miss Monti's like a breath of fresh Alaskan air!" she would breathe happily, blue eyes sparkling in a porcelain doll's face. Eulah Mae was glad to see Miss Tish happy, like she was now. From above, she could hear her light, airy laughter blending in with Miss Monti's hearty guffaw.

The last of the dishes were put up, and supper was in the oven. There wasn't much more for her to do. She decided to dust the dining room again. Getting the cloth, she thought about Miss Tish and how she didn't treat her like a servant. They talked and laughed easily together, and sometimes when it was blazing hot, Miss Tish would have her rest on the veranda with her and sip a cool drink. At one of those times, she confided in Miss Tish about working long enough to save money to go away to nursing school. Miss Tish was encouraging, saying that schooling was important. Then, laughing deprecatingly, she added, "What good did going to Ward-Belmont do for me!" The next week Miss Tish raised her salary to ten dollars a week.

Eulah Mae dusted where there was no dust. The rest of the day, she occupied herself with manufacturing chores to do. At six o'clock, time for her to go, she did as usual when Miss Tish didn't come down before she left. She wrote a note about supper. The salad was in the ice box, and the roast and potatoes in the oven. It had grown quiet upstairs, as if Miss Tish and Miss Monti were asleep. The silence came down to her like a dirge of strangeness. Quietly she locked the door behind her.

II

"You mean you just upped and left like *that!* Without letting her *know?*" Louella asked, sitting across from Eulah Mae at the rickety wooden kitchen table, back to the door stretched wide to let out the kitchen heat.

"I always do," Eulah Mae said, regretting the detailing of her workday with Louella, who could make a mountain out of a mole hill. She set the warmed-over chicken and dumplings, crowder peas and cold water corn bread on the table. Louella had stopped by on the way home from the ammunition factory and stayed, without too much urging, to eat.

Louella had quit school in the seventh grade to go to work, but she and Eulah Mae remained friends throughout the years. Both were as different as day and night. Louella was more outgoing and worldly-wise. Her easygoing ways and quickness for laughter collected many friends, unlike Eulah Mae's shy reserve, which made her a loner.

Generously helping herself to the food, Louella asked slyly, "Wonder what they doin' upstairs alone like that all the time?"

"Talking . . ."

"Hah!" Louella sniggered, choking slightly on the corn bread, eyes wide. "They *talkin'*, I bet. They say that Miss Monti's one of them funny women."

Eulah Mae stared down at the red checked oilcloth covering the table, face knotted in a puzzled frown. "I don't believe that . . ."

" 'Course, it don't make no dif'frence to *me,* long's she ain't after what *I* got!" Louella laughed explosively. "Lots of women, I hear, in the city turnin' funny since most of the men done gone off to the war. We even got a few workin' in the fac'try. They look and dress just like men in those old overhalls and heavy shoes. I stay clear of them myself. Don't want none of them messin' 'round with *me.* They say that once you do, you don't never want another man. I'm scared of them!"

Eulah Mae felt warmth consuming her, heated by surprise and the excitement of the shocking sexual topic. What could women *do* together? She was ashamed of the talk about Miss Monti. Miss Tish's friend was nice to her, called her Miss Brown, and gave her rides home. Her thoughts lingered like stone on the funny women Louella spoke of.

"Why you so quiet all of a sudden? One of them ever say anythin' to *you?*" Louella giggled.

Mouth tight, Eulah Mae began to scrape up the dishes, wanting to end the subject that made her uncomfortable. "Like some dessert? Leftover apple pie I made for Miss Tish Sunday."

"Uh-huh. Give me some of Miss Tish's leftover pie!" Louella sneered derisively. Watching Eulah Mae slicing the dessert, she said quietly, "Why don't you quit workin' for that white woman and come with us to the fac'try? Make more money for that nursin' school you so set on goin' to."

"Have to get up too early," Eulah Mae replied hastily. Riding all the way to Spring City on a crowded old bus to work beside strangers in a place filled with noise and supervision terrified her. At Miss Tish's she didn't have to punch a clock, worked at her own pace, and without the factory clamor.

"You'd be doin' your bit for the war effort," Louella pressed on. "Helpin' the boys over there. We got some need helpin', too, workin' at the fac'try with me," she laughed, "even if they is 4-F's! Pretty as you are, you could git one in no time."

Eulah Mae remained silent, eyes on her food. Men had never been uppermost in her mind. Not even her father, who left when she was eight years old and never came back.

Louella wiped her mouth with a paper napkin. "Hum-m-m, that was sure good. Glad I stayed."

"I am, too."

"Eulah Mae . . ." Louella's voice softened. "You and me been friends a long time, and I'm gittin' worried 'bout you."

"Me . . . why?"

" 'Cause you too young to be doin' nothin' but goin' to work and comin' home to eat and sleep and go back to work again." She paused reflectively. "I know you got a goal in mind, wantin' to go back to school and make somethin' more of yourself, but you ought to git out and have some fun while you young and *can*." Sighing, Louella shook her head. " 'Course you ain't never been much of a fun type."

Eulah Mae turned the invitation over in her mind. A movie would be a change. "All right . . ." The answer slipped out on its own.

"Good!" Louella smiled triumphantly. "I'll come by for you 'round seven. OK?"

Eulah Mae nodded, looking beyond the brightness in Louella's eyes. Already she was sorry that she had agreed to go.

III

Elevated high in the loft of the crow's nest above the white people, Eulah Mae and Louella saw Ginger Rogers and Fred Astaire. One time Louella maliciously threw popcorn below to let *them* know how she felt about having to sit in the "For Colored" section.

When the movie was over, laughing together like two carefree school girls, they walked down Main Street, passing the brightly lit ice cream parlor where the young white teenagers gathered around the jukebox in bobby socks and saddle shoes listening to Glenn Miller's orchestra. The parlor only offered carry-out service for colored people. They went by without looking in.

"Let's go to The Hole for a beer," Louella suggested. "It's hot and I'm thirsty."

Eulah Mae hesitated, for she had never been to The Hole before, a place her mother called a "den of iniquity." Besides, she didn't like beer.

Sensing her hesitancy, Louella added quickly, "We won't stay long."

The Hole was a long, flat-roofed, barrackslike stone building with a tin, makeshift sign in front. It was crowded as usual with Saturday night revelers, for there wasn't anywhere else for colored to go. The loud music box blared with Billy Eckstine's baritone singing about jelly, jelly, jelly staying on his mind. The place was semi-dark, but Louella could apparently see without difficulty, for she recognized friends, calling out gaily to them.

"Hey . . . Mary Lee! Oh-o-o, Willie!" She stopped to hug a tall, lean man in a black zoot suit with a gold watch chain dangling from his pocket.

"Hi, Louella, baby!" He pecked a kiss on her cheek.

"Willie, this here's my friend, Eulah Mae . . ."

Willie squinted appreciatively at Eulah Mae. "My . . . my. I'd sure like to have a friend like *that!* What ya'll drinkin'?"

"Since you buyin', two rum cokes with cherries," Louella laughed.

"Che-e-ries?" Willie winked meaningfully, turning away.

Army uniforms swelled the crowd, for Camp Breckinridge wasn't too far away. Watching a young corporal pass, Louella licked her lips. "Hum-m-m, I just lo-o-ve my men in uniform. Don't you? Makes them look so man-n-ly!" Grabbing Eulah Mae's hand, she said, "Let's sit over here."

They sat at a small, round table, jammed against others with arms and backs brushing theirs in grazing movements.

"Here we go! Two drinks for two sharp chicks . . ." Willie set the glasses down. "Now, Eulah Mae, sugar, wanna dance?"

It had been a while since she had danced. The last time was at the high school prom.

"G'wan and dance with Willie," Louella prompted.

Reluctantly she went into his open arms of cigarette smoke and whisky smells. Holding her airtight close, they danced on a dime to Erskine Hawkin's "Tuxedo Junction."

"Where's a sweet thing like you been hidin' out 'round here, baby? I'd sure like to see more of you."

While Willie tried to make time, she mentally disconnected him, looking over his humped shoulders around the room. The bar was surrounded with drinkers, except for one end where a solitary figure sat alone, arched over a beer and ash tray of burned down cigarettes, separated by two stools from the others. Peering closer in the dimness, she saw that it was a woman with short, wavy hair slicked back from a light, flat, empty-looking face.

Turning abruptly to survey the room, the woman's eyes met hers and stayed to follow her in the locked arms of Willie. When he kissed her neck, a slight smile of amusement grazed the woman's mouth at her discomfort. Embarrassed by the woman watching them, Eulah Mae pushed Willie away, leaving him standing on the floor gaping after her.

"Why'd you do that, baby? Just when it was gettin' go-o-od," he sneered loudly.

Their table was vacant. Louella was dancing with a soldier. She sat down, then looked up to see the shadowy figure of the woman at the bar standing over her. The woman wore a man's starched white shirt opened at the collar and gray, pegged pants with a zipper in the front.

"Mind if I sit down?" she asked, voice hoarse with entreatment.

"You damn right she does!" Louella snapped harshly, returning. *"Git, bulldagger!"*

The woman's face swelled with pain and rage. Her mouth opened as if to give a retort, then closed tightly. Glancing at Eulah Mae, she shrugged and went back to the bar in long, stiff strides. The crowd parted for her like the Red Sea.

"She's one of *them* I was tellin' you 'bout . . ." Louella said, sitting down scowling. "The *nerve* of her comin' over here like that!"

Eulah Mae frowned at the bar where the woman, who was supposed to be one of *them,* sat isolated on the stool. Eulah Mae saw her sharply strike a match against a square match box to light a cigarette over a fresh beer. Somehow, she could sense the woman's loneliness on her island apart.

"What happened 'tween you and Willie?" Louella picked up her drink. "He's 4-F, but a nice guy. Makes good money as a foreman at the fac'try."

Eulah Mae got up, squeezing away from the boxed-in table, bumping arms and legs. "I'm going home . . ."

"What for? It's early yet . . ." Louella looked surprised and hurt.

"You stay. Have fun. I enjoyed the movie . . ." she amended, hoping it would allay the rudeness of leaving. This wasn't the place for her.

On the way out, she paused ever so briefly at the end of the bar to whisper a "Goodnight" to the woman whom she had almost met.

IV

When the spring flowed into summer, Mr. Southerland, who had become Lieutenant Southerland, was sent overseas. Soon, Miss Monti began to practically live at the house. It was a common sight for Eulah Mae to see her and Miss Tish strolling hand-in-hand through the flower garden, withdrawn into a world of their own.

Miss Tish's face had taken on a shiny glow, cheeks fired with a warm, rosy color, and her blue eyes sparkled with a brightness not seen before. She was blossoming like the flowers nourished by her tender care. They were obviously good for each other.

Oftentimes when Eulah Mae went home in the evenings, she left Miss Monti still at the house. She knew by the bag that Miss Monti was staying overnight; however, the following mornings, there was only one bed to be made. Sometimes on weekends, Miss Monti and Miss Tish would drive to Louisville in the Packard to shop, see friends, and get away from the sticks for a while, they told her.

The Monday after Thanksgiving it happened. Coming back from Louisville for the holidays, Miss Monti's car rounded a curve too fast on the icy road outside of town and crashed into a tree. Miss Monti was killed instantly.

Miss Tish was rushed to the hospital with internal injuries. It was a week until anyone could visit her. The army gave Lieutenant Southerland a leave to fly back to be with his wife. He had changed, looking older, eyes puffed in a haggard face, gray shading his temples, but he carried himself haughty and southern proud in his uniform. Nervous and jumpy, he was not very patient with Miss Tish when she came home from the hospital. The air of wanting to leave, get back someplace else, showed in his brusque mannerisms with people and things about him. He drank more than usual, almost consuming a fifth of bourbon a day.

"Eulah Mae . . ." he said to her one morning in the kitchen, mixing his before breakfast bourbon and water, "I can't conceive of somebody getting killed and injuring another person because of being too damn stupid to drive carefully on a slippery road at night. Men are gettin killed for more than that where I came from!"

To Eulah Mae, it was like he had no pity at all. While he brooded and drank, Miss Tish lay silently in the big, four-poster bed where her mother had given birth to her, eyes a cloudy mist on the gold, flowered wallpaper.

"Well, I'm off to win the war!" Lieutenant Southerland announced unexpectedly one day, packing his bag. Setting his officer's cap at a jaunty angle over his eyes, he appeared relieved. "Take care of her, Eulah Mae. Miss Tish needs you."

Miss Tish did not react one way or another to his leaving. It was like he hadn't been there. When he left, Eulah Mae moved into the once live-in maid's room to be near Miss Tish at all times. There were nights when Miss Tish couldn't sleep, and wanted her to stay with her while she read or simply stay still, eyes closed, while thoughts flailed her mind like gray rain. Sitting in the rocker beside her, Eulah Mae sewed, rocked, and cast anxious glances at the pencil-slim figure in the bed.

Once, Miss Tish looked at her, eyes wide and vacant, to say, "I *told* her to slow down. She was so impetuous. Like an untamed pony. But I loved her for it. Oh, Monti . . . Monti . . ."

Miss Tish cried and Eulah Mae held her hand, cold and dry like a fall leaf. Tenderly she wiped the tears away and the dampness from her forehead. Quietly Eulah Mae, too, grieved with her mistress.

Winter faded and spring crept in on the winged tips of warm breezes. Miss Tish began to get out of bed and move around to get her strength back.

Friends came to visit again, but Eulah Mae was her sole intimate companion and bed of rock. In the day, they walked side by side among the colorful array of flowers, and in the evenings, they talked read, and listened to the radio in the parlor upstairs. Off and on, a cloud would fill Miss Tish's eyes, darkening them, but was blinked away.

The evenings grew longer and Miss Tish's spirits livened under blue skies warmed by the sun. Sometimes, when together alone in the house or walking outside, Miss Tish would reach for Eulah Mae's hand, hold it for a light moment, then release it like a feather, face closed in a secret smile.

The telegram came on a gray, chilly April day. Lieutenant Southerland had been killed in action. The army brought him home for burial. The day of the funeral, the canning factory closed, and the flag over the courthouse was lowered at half mast in honor of the town's fallen warrior.

Miss Tish stood up gallantly under the stress, stoically taking the flag expertly folded and handed to her by the honor guard. When the body was lowered into the ground, she stared over the tops of the marble grave markers into the shoal of clouds. The sound of taps emptied the message of death into the stillness.

At home alone with Eulah Mae in the stately old house soaked with memories, Miss Tish cried. Eulah Mae discovered the tears were not for her husband, but Miss Monti. "It was all brought back again, Eulah Mae. Just think, I wasn't even able to go to her funeral!"

Eulah Mae made Miss Tish a hot toddy and put her to bed. When Miss Tish finally went to sleep, she remained awake in her small room, thoughts alive with the news brought to her that day. She had been accepted to Meharry for the fall. Now the excitement had begun to ebb at leaving Miss Tish. Especially with Lieutenant Southerland dead. Miss Tish had grown so frail, weakened in mind and spirit. She was eight years younger than Miss Tish, but the stronger of the two. Did work and life make black women stronger?

The day after Lieutenant Southerland's funeral, Miss Tish started to follow Eulah Mae around the house as she performed her chores. Miss Tish seemed fearful of letting Eulah Mae out of her sight, eyes devouring her every movement. Trailing beside her, Miss Tish's arm would go lightly about her waist as she talked aimlessly, or her fingertips would graze her arm like she had meant to take it but changed her mind.

Frequently when their eyes met, Miss Tish's would trap Eulah Mae's in a vise and hold until Eulah Mae, flustered, would tear hers away. Eulah Mae was reminded of how Miss Tish and Miss Monti used to look at each other, and a shiver would run down her spine as thin as a thumbnail.

Eulah Mae put off telling Miss Tish about going away to school. Each day, the two of them grew closer and closer, secreted in the monastic seclusion of their existence. Gradually, they became imprisoned in a tangled web of need and giving. Taking care of Miss Tish to Eulah Mae had grown to be virtue. She was ministering to one who depended upon her, and Miss Tish flowered beneath her care like she had with Miss Monti's nurturing.

Sitting beside Miss Tish propped up in bed one warm August night, Eulah Mae tried to form the words about leaving. They were stopped when Miss Tish put down the book she was reading to reach for her hand. A faint breeze came through the window, fluttering the curtains in a shimmering dance of lace.

"You're the best friend I have now, Eulah Mae . . ." Miss Tish's voice came out light and thin. "I depend on you a lot, don't I?"

Eulah Mae's hand grew damp, clasped in the warmth of Miss Tish's holding hers. "Not that much, Miss Tish . . ." she said softly.

"Oh, but I do!" Miss Tish exclaimed, face in a veil of truth. "You're so *kind* to me, Eulah Mae, so gentle . . ." Then, almost like perceiving what had been on Eulah Mae's mind, "If you leave me, I don't know what I'd do. I *need* you, Eulah Mae. We've become so close . . . a different kind of closeness, haven't we?"

Eulah Mae couldn't answer, a constriction sealing her throat. She stared at the darkness of her hand against the whiteness of Miss Tish's, which was softer than hers, not hardened by work. There were the two of them, bound together in an uncommon affinity of servant and mistress, black and white, whose roles had become distorted in this southern time. She had forgotten what she was in their isolated milieu of oneness.

Miss Tish's hand tightened. "You're very pretty, Eulah Mae," she added huskily. "I'm afraid someone will take you away from me." Miss Tish leaned near, eyes glowing in a strange way, like a cat's charming a bird. "I've grown very fond of you, Eulah Mae. You've become a part of me, and I, of you."

The room suddenly seemed too stuffy and warm. Eulah Mae's hand went limp and sweaty in Miss Tish's clasp. She was unable to say anything. When Miss Tish shifted to draw closer, she could smell the lilac perfume and see the cleft of the white, puffy breasts halfway hidden in the yellow nightgown. A trickle of moisture dotted the pink blade of Miss Tish's mouth.

Suddenly the sharp, heavy squall of the air raid siren lashed the silence between them. Practices were becoming more frequent. "I've got to close the blinds . . ." Eulah Mae felt her words thick and chalky in her mouth.

When she returned, the voice from the bed was low and engulfing. "Now, turn off the lights, too, Eulah Mae, and come back here to me."

Switching off the lights, she found her way without difficulty in the darkness to the bed. The path was as familiar to her as her face.

The next order was hushed, but strong as the wind of a gale. "Undress and get in here with me, Eulah Mae."

Looking down on Miss Tish's face gleaming whitely in the darkness, the vision of the woman in the bar eclipsed her thoughts like a flash of lightning. Mesmerized, she slipped off her robe and eased into the bed. The sheets were cool against her flushed body.

Miss Tish's arms stretched like slender wings to seal her within. Her pliant breasts pressed into Eulah Mae's, crushing her. "Eulah Mae, I want to be with you . . . like this! Don't be frightened, it's all right . . ." White hands moved slowly over brown curves of flesh, creating tiny patches of fire. "You won't leave me, Eulah Mae. Will you, ever?"

Eulah Mae felt smothered against the softness and warmth and flood of desire. Her answer was buried against the lips of Miss Tish. Trembling, she closed her eyes. She realized that she would never leave. She couldn't . . . now. The silence answered for her.

A few of the publications of
THE NAIAD PRESS, INC.
P.O. Box 10543 • Tallahassee, Florida 32302
Phone (904) 539-9322
Mail orders welcome. Please include 15% postage.

THE BLACK AND WHITE OF IT by Ann Allen Shockley. 144 pp. Short stories.   ISBN 0-930044-96-7 $7.95

SAY JESUS AND COME TO ME by Ann Allen Shockley. 288 pp. Contemporary romance.   ISBN 0-930044-98-3   8.95

LOVING HER by Ann Allen Shockley. 192 pp. Romantic love story.   ISBN 0-930044-97-5   7.95

MURDER AT THE NIGHTWOOD BAR by Katherine V. Forrest. 240 pp. A Kate Delafield mystery. Second in a series.
ISBN 0-930044-92-4   8.95

ZOE'S BOOK by Gail Pass. 224 pp. Passionate, obsessive love story.   ISBN 0-930044-95-9   7.95

WINGED DANCER by Camarin Grae. 228 pp. Erotic Lesbian adventure story.   ISBN 0-930044-88-6   8.95

PAZ by Camarin Grae. 336 pp. Romantic Lesbian adventurer with the power to change the world. ISBN 0-930044-89-4   8.95

SOUL SNATCHER by Camarin Grae. 224 pp. A puzzle, an adventure, a mystery—Lesbian romance. ISBN 0-930044-90-8   8.95

THE LOVE OF GOOD WOMEN by Isabel Miller. 224 pp. Long-awaited new novel by the author of the beloved *Patience and Sarah*.   ISBN 0-930044-81-9   8.95

THE HOUSE AT PELHAM FALLS by Brenda Weathers. 240 pp. Suspenseful Lesbian ghost story.   ISBN 0-930044-79-7   7.95

HOME IN YOUR HANDS by Lee Lynch. 240 pp. More stories from the author of *Old Dyke Tales*.   ISBN 0-930044-80-0   7.95

EACH HAND A MAP by Anita Skeen. 112 pp. Real-life poems that touch us all.   ISBN 0-930044-82-7   6.95

SURPLUS by Sylvia Stevenson. 342 pp. A classic early Lesbian novel.   ISBN 0-930044-78-9   7.95

PEMBROKE PARK by Michelle Martin. 256 pp. Derring-do and daring romance in Regency England. ISBN 0-930044-77-0   7.95

THE LONG TRAIL by Penny Hayes. 248 pp. Vivid adventures of two women in love in the old west. ISBN 0-930044-76-2   8.95

HORIZON OF THE HEART by Shelley Smith. 192 pp. Hot romance in summertime New England.   ISBN 0-930044-75-4   7.95

AN EMERGENCE OF GREEN by Katherine V. Forrest. 288 pp. Powerful novel of sexual discovery.   ISBN 0-930044-69-X   8.95

THE LESBIAN PERIODICALS INDEX edited by Claire Potter. 432 pp. Author & subject index. ISBN 0-930044-74-6   29.95

DESERT OF THE HEART by Jane Rule. 224 pp. A classic; basis for the movie *Desert Hearts*.   ISBN 0-930044-73-8   7.95

SPRING FORWARD/FALL BACK by Sheila Ortiz Taylor. 288 pp. Literary novel of timeless love.   ISBN 0-930044-70-3   7.95

FOR KEEPS by Elisabeth Nonas. 144 pp. Contemporary novel about losing and finding love.   ISBN 0-930044-71-1   7.95

TORCHLIGHT TO VALHALLA by Gale Wilhelm. 128 pp. Classic novel by a great Lesbian writer.   ISBN 0-930044-68-1   7.95

LESBIAN NUNS: BREAKING SILENCE edited by Rosemary Curb and Nancy Manahan. 432 pp. Unprecedented autobiographies of religious life. ISBN 0-930044-62-2 9.95

THE SWASHBUCKLER by Lee Lynch. 288 pp. Colorful novel set in Greenwich Village in the sixties. ISBN 0-930044-66-5 7.95

MISFORTUNE'S FRIEND by Sarah Aldridge. 320 pp. Historical Lesbian novel set on two continents. ISBN 0-930044-67-3 7.95

A STUDIO OF ONE'S OWN by Ann Stokes. Edited by Dolores Klaich. 128 pp. Autobiography. ISBN 0-930044-64-9 7.95

SEX VARIANT WOMEN IN LITERATURE by Jeannette Howard Foster. 448 pp. Literary history. ISBN 0-930044-65-7 8.95

A HOT-EYED MODERATE by Jane Rule. 252 pp. Hard-hitting essays on gay life; writing; art. ISBN 0-930044-57-6 7.95

INLAND PASSAGE AND OTHER STORIES by Jane Rule. 288 pp. Wide-ranging new collection. ISBN 0-930044-56-8 7.95

WE TOO ARE DRIFTING by Gale Wilhelm. 128 pp. Timeless Lesbian novel, a masterpiece. ISBN 0-930044-61-4 6.95

AMATEUR CITY by Katherine V. Forrest. 224 pp. A Kate Delafield mystery. First in a series. ISBN 0-930044-55-X 7.95

THE SOPHIE HOROWITZ STORY by Sarah Schulman. 176 pp. Engaging novel of madcap intrigue. ISBN 0-930044-54-1 7.95

THE BURNTON WIDOWS by Vicki P. McConnell. 272 pp. A Nyla Wade mystery, second in the series. ISBN 0-930044-52-5 7.95

OLD DYKE TALES by Lee Lynch. 224 pp. Extraordinary stories of our diverse Lesbian lives. ISBN 0-930044-51-7 7.95

DAUGHTERS OF A CORAL DAWN by Katherine V. Forrest. 240 pp. Novel set in a Lesbian new world. ISBN 0-930044-50-9 7.95

THE PRICE OF SALT by Claire Morgan. 288 pp. A milestone novel, a beloved classic. ISBN 0-930044-49-5 8.95

AGAINST THE SEASON by Jane Rule. 224 pp. Luminous, complex novel of interrelationships. ISBN 0-930044-48-7 7.95

LOVERS IN THE PRESENT AFTERNOON by Kathleen Fleming. 288 pp. A novel about recovery and growth. ISBN 0-930044-46-0 8.50

TOOTHPICK HOUSE by Lee Lynch. 264 pp. Love between two Lesbians of different classes. ISBN 0-930044-45-2 7.95

MADAME AURORA by Sarah Aldridge. 256 pp. Historical novel featuring a charismatic "seer." ISBN 0-930044-44-4 7.95

CURIOUS WINE by Katherine V. Forrest. 176 pp. Passionate Lesbian love story, a best-seller. ISBN 0-930044-43-6 7.95

BLACK LESBIAN IN WHITE AMERICA by Anita Cornwell. 141 pp. Stories, essays, autobiography. ISBN 0-930044-41-X 7.50

CONTRACT WITH THE WORLD by Jane Rule. 340 pp. Powerful, panoramic novel of gay life. ISBN 0-930044-28-2 7.95

YANTRAS OF WOMANLOVE by Tee A. Corinne. 64 pp. Photos by noted Lesbian photographer. ISBN 0-930044-30-4 6.95

MRS. PORTER'S LETTER by Vicki P. McConnell. 224 pp. The first Nyla Wade mystery. ISBN 0-930044-29-0 7.95

TO THE CLEVELAND STATION by Carol Anne Douglas. 192 pp. Interracial Lesbian love story. ISBN 0-930044-27-4 6.95

THE NESTING PLACE by Sarah Aldridge. 224 pp. Historical novel, a three-woman triangle. ISBN 0-930044-26-6 7.95

THIS IS NOT FOR YOU by Jane Rule. 284 pp. A letter to a
beloved is also an intricate novel.   ISBN 0-930044-25-8   7.95

FAULTLINE by Sheila Ortiz Taylor. 140 pp. Warm, funny,
literate story of a startling family.   ISBN 0-930044-24-X   6.95

THE LESBIAN IN LITERATURE by Barbara Grier. 3d ed.
Foreword by Maida Tilchen. 240 pp. Comprehensive bibliography. Literary ratings; rare photos.   ISBN 0-930044-23-1   7.95

ANNA'S COUNTRY by Elizabeth Lang. 208 pp. A woman
finds her Lesbian identity.   ISBN 0-930044-19-3   6.95

PRISM by Valerie Taylor. 158 pp. A love affair between two
women in their sixties.   ISBN 0-930044-18-5   6.95

BLACK LESBIANS: AN ANNOTATED BIBLIOGRAPHY
compiled by J.R. Roberts. Foreword by Barbara Smith. 112
pp. Award winning bibliography.   ISBN 0-930044-21-5   5.95

THE MARQUISE AND THE NOVICE by Victoria Ramstetter.
108 pp. A Lesbian Gothic novel.   ISBN 0-930044-16-9   4.95

LABIAFLOWERS by Tee A. Corinne. 40 pp. Drawings by the
noted artist/photographer.   ISBN 0-930044-20-7   3.95

OUTLANDER by Jane Rule. 207 pp. Short stories and essays
by one of our finest writers.   ISBN 0-930044-17-7   6.95

SAPPHISTRY: THE BOOK OF LESBIAN SEXUALITY by
Pat Califia. 2d edition, revised. 195 pp.   ISBN 0-930044-47-9   7.95

ALL TRUE LOVERS by Sarah Aldridge. 292 pp. Romantic
novel set in the 1930s and 1940s.   ISBN 0-930044-10-X   7.95

A WOMAN APPEARED TO ME by Renee Vivien. 65 pp. A
classic; translated by Jeannette H. Foster. ISBN 0-930044-06-1   5.00

CYTHEREA'S BREATH by Sarah Aldridge. 240 pp. Women
first enter medicine and the law: a novel. ISBN 0-930044-02-9   6.95

TOTTIE by Sarah Aldridge. 181 pp. Lesbian romance in the
turmoil of the sixties.   ISBN 0-930044-01-0   6.95

THE LATECOMER by Sarah Aldridge. 107 pp. A delicate love
story set in days gone by.   ISBN 0-930044-00-2   5.00

ODD GIRL OUT by Ann Bannon   ISBN 0-930044-83-5   5.95
I AM A WOMAN by Ann Bannon.   ISBN 0-930044-84-3   5.95
WOMEN IN THE SHADOWS by Ann Bannon.
                                      ISBN 0-930044-85-1   5.95
JOURNEY TO A WOMAN by Ann Bannon.
                                      ISBN 0-930044-86-X   5.95
BEEBO BRINKER by Ann Bannon   ISBN 0-930044-87-8   5.95
         Legendary novels written in the fifties and sixties,
              set in the gay mecca of Greenwich Village.

VOLUTE BOOKS

JOURNEY TO FULFILLMENT	Early classics by Valerie	3.95
A WORLD WITHOUT MEN	Taylor: The Erika Frohmann	3.95
RETURN TO LESBOS	series.	3.95

These are just a few of the many Naiad Press titles—we are the oldest and largest lesbian/feminist publishing company in the world. Please request a complete catalog. We offer personal service; we encourage and welcome direct mail orders from individuals who have limited access to bookstores carrying our publications.